It took Sam a while to realize that a war was going on, and that it had been declared in the Easter term of Year Eleven. The first he knew about it was the morning he woke up tired and washed-out. When he got out of bed, he felt as if his bones had been recast in lead . . .

Sam doesn't know it but this is the moment when his war – to stay alive – begins.

And nearly a hundred years in the past, another Sam is also about to go to war – on the Western Front . . .

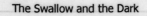

Also by Andrew Matthews,
published by Random House Children's Books:

THE BREAKFAST MUSEUM
FROM ABOVE WITH LOVE
G.S.O.H.

The
SWALLOW
and the
DARK

ANDREW MATTHEWS

CORGI BOOKS

THE SWALLOW AND THE DARK
A CORGI BOOK 0 552 55229 1

First publication in Great Britain

Corgi edition published 2005

1 3 5 7 9 10 8 6 4 2

Set in AGaramond by Palimpsest Book Production Ltd,
Polmont, Stirlingshire

Corgi Books are published by Random House Children's Books,
61–63 Uxbridge Road, London W5 5SA,
a division of The Random House Group Ltd,
in Australia by Random House Australia (Pty) Ltd,
20 Alfred Street, Milsons Point, Sydney, NSW 2061, Australia,
in New Zealand by Random House New Zealand Ltd,
18 Poland Road, Glenfield, Auckland 10, New Zealand,
and in South Africa by Random House (Pty) Ltd,
Endulini, 5A Jubilee Road, Parktown 2193, South Africa

THE RANDOM HOUSE GROUP Limited Reg. No. 954009
www.kidsatrandomhouse.co.uk

A CIP catalogue record for this book is available from the British Library.

Printed and bound in Great Britain by
Cox & Wyman Ltd, Reading, Berkshire

In memory of the cousin I never knew
JIMMY WELLS
Killed in action, 1944

PART ONE

One

Sam Rawnsley hadn't been expecting any kind of mystical experience, especially not at school, but that was right where it happened. Sam was in Year Ten at the time – a Thursday morning in October – and in the English suite. Outside the classroom it was dank and a thick mist curled against the windows; inside it was warm, with the fuzzy feel of a classful of teens who weren't fully awake yet and hoped that Mr Prince wouldn't ask them to do anything too strenuous, such as thinking.

Sam was drifting in a daydream, knowing that he could take it anywhere that he wanted. At some level he was aware of Mr Prince talking about the First World War, and idly wondered what that was supposed to have to do with English, but he wasn't curious enough to concentrate.

Then Mr Prince began to read out a poem, and Sam got lost. The poem yanked him through a loophole in reality and swallowed him. He lurched through a darkness lit by flares that cast sweeping shadows around him as they fell. He heard men coughing and cursing, smelled a choking sweetness that brought bile to the back of his throat; a man on his right cried out and pitched forwards . . .

And Sam came back, blinking at the vinyl surface of the table in front of him, shaken by a memory that was impossible because it concerned events that had occurred long before he had been born.

What, Sam thought, was *that*?

He'd thought that he only knew what most people knew about the First World War – trenches, gas, poppies, the poster of the guy with the big moustache – but the poem had made him aware that there was more to the war, and more to himself.

Never one to dip a toe into the water when he could dive in headfirst, Sam immersed himself in research. He watched TV documentaries, surfed the net, borrowed books from the library and came up with more information than he could handle, but none of it seemed real. The historians all had axes to grind, still playing blame-games after almost a century, and the TV programmes and websites were dumbed-down and unsatisfying. Only poetry could recapture what Sam had experienced in the English lesson – the fear, the anger, the sense of betrayal.

Whose betrayal? thought Sam. When have you ever been betrayed?

Eventually Sam's passion for the First World War faded, but it never completely vanished. It returned to him in dreams, flashes of imagination that could be triggered without warning. Sam didn't worry about it. It was all just part of the general weirdness of growing up and studying GCSEs. In fact, compared to some of the other people in Sam's year, having a thing about the First World War was no big deal.

It took Sam a while to realize that a war was going on, and that it had been declared in the Easter term of Year Eleven. The first he knew about it was the morning he woke up tired and washed-out. When he got out of bed, he felt as if his bones had been recast in lead.

'It's like having a hangover without having had the fun part first,' he told his mother over breakfast.

She gave him one of her sharp looks and said, 'And how would you know what a hangover's like?'

Sam thought, Oops!

He said, 'I *imagine* this is what a hangover's like.'

Mum pressed her right hand to his forehead.

'You're not running a temperature,' she said suspiciously. 'Is everything all right at school?'

Great! thought Sam. Now she thinks I'm faking it to get out of something. He said, 'Everything at school is fine. I just don't feel so good, that's all.'

Actually, things at school weren't fine, because Sam had recently discovered that the vague crush he had on Jade Simpson, one of the girls in his English group, was in fact full-on passionate love. Unfortunately, Jade was in a deep-and-meaningful with Simon Tomlinson, and wouldn't give Sam the time of day. If he suddenly ceased to exist, he doubted that Jade would notice. Even his fantasies about her were hopeless. He'd once imagined himself with Jade in his front room, listening to music. Jade had been elegantly sprawled on the sofa, and Sam had been seated at her feet, holding her hand. Jade had looked at him, smiled and said, 'You know this is only a daydream, don't you? It would never ever happen in real life.'

But Jade wasn't the reason he felt so lousy that morning.

The following Friday, the war entered a new phase and Sam passed out for the first time. He was in assembly, pretending to listen to the announcements that his Year Head was making, when all of a sudden the world began to fade and grew so thin that Sam fell right through it into big black nowhere. He came to in the medical room and threw up into a wastepaper bin.

The school nurse gave him some tissues to wipe his mouth.

'Has this happened before?' she asked.

'No,' said Sam.

'Have you had any dizzy spells, severe headaches or anything like that?'

Sam shook his head and wished that he hadn't – the room went on yawing from side to side after his head was still.

'No,' he said.

'How d'you react to strobe lights?'

'I usually go – *Wow, strobe lights!*' said Sam.

This didn't go down too well. The nurse's eyes hardened.

'There's a nasty virus around at the moment,' she said. 'You should make an appointment with your doctor. Is anyone at home?'

Sam bristled with resentment. What am I, ten years old or something? he thought. He said, 'My mum's at work.'

'And your father?'

'My parents are divorced.'

It was funny how, even after three years, it still hurt like a paper-cut to say it.

'Would you like me to call your mother to come and pick you up?'

'No,' said Sam. 'I'll be all right.'

8

The last thing he needed was his mother fussing around. Fainting in front of everybody in Year Eleven was humiliating enough to be going on with, and Sam began concocting a story to cover it. When his mates asked him, he'd say that Mum had gone out the night before, and he'd got off his face on half a bottle of vodka. He pictured himself leaving the house, walking down to the parade of shops in Whitgift Avenue, heard the buzzer of the off-licence door sounding as he went in, saw money changing hands, then followed a quick stroll to the benches near the tennis courts on the Green for some serious boozing.

And then I dumped the empty bottle in the pond and chucked stones at it until it smashed, he thought. Yeah, I like that. Nice touch.

It was such a nice touch that by the time he left the medical room, Sam had almost convinced himself that it had actually happened.

He had hoped to avoid telling his mother about the fainting, but he had to when he threw up again after dinner. She gave him a grilling that he could really have done without: What had he been eating?

What had he been drinking? Then she got on to drugs.

'You know how I feel about drugs, Sam.'

'Yes, Mum.'

'I won't tolerate that sort of thing.'

'No, Mum.'

'If you've been taking drugs—'

'I haven't, Mum.'

Which was true. Sam had always been too scared, afraid that his mind might get to a place there was no way out of. He had what English teachers described as 'a vivid imagination'. Sam called it 'drifting' because his imagination would go off for hours at a time and he'd go with it, drifting like a jellyfish in an ocean current. Anything could trigger it – a boring lesson, a cloud, the play of sunlight on water. Music was especially strong. Sam only had to hear a snatch of classical music, and his imagination turned it into a movie in his head.

Mum muttered something to herself about rescheduling, then said, 'Right! First thing on Monday morning, I'm taking you to the doctor.'

'There's no need to bother the doctor,' Sam said.

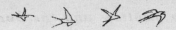

'It's just a stomach bug. It'll be gone by Monday.'

'You're going to the doctor,' Mum insisted.

Sam didn't object. He was too tired to argue.

In the surgery on Monday morning, Dr Robertson listened to Sam's chest, took his pulse, temperature and blood pressure, looked down his throat and shone a light into his ears and eyes.

'A low-grade viral infection,' he said, scribbling out a prescription. 'Take these tablets three times a day, after meals. Stay home and rest. If you're not feeling any better at the end of the week, make another appointment. Keep warm and drink plenty of fluids.'

'What else would I drink?' Sam said.

Dr Robertson frowned. 'I'm sorry?'

'You told me to drink fluids,' Sam explained. 'How could I drink anything else *but* fluids?'

Dr Robertson's mouth lengthened into a smile. 'Oh, I see!' he said. 'You've a sharp wit, Sam. Careful you don't cut yourself on it.' He put on a pair of rubber gloves, took a cloth off a stainless steel kidney-dish and picked up a hypodermic.

'What's that for?' said Sam, alarmed.

'I want to take a blood sample, just to be sure,' said Dr Robertson. 'Purely routine, nothing for you to worry about.'

Sam wasn't worried about the sample, it was having a needle stuck in his arm that concerned him.

The needle stung.

Sam spent most of the next two days asleep. A couple of his mates called round to see him, and he could hardly keep his eyes open. His dream life was far more intriguing than reality. In dreams he wasn't quite someone else, but he wasn't himself either. Dream Sam walked along city streets and was bewildered by what he saw. Buildings were box-like and soul-less; traffic was deafening and smelled awful; people wore strange clothes and spoke so quickly that he couldn't catch their meaning. Dream Sam found the world as alien as if he'd beamed-down from another planet, and when Sam woke from such dreams, for a while the world seemed alien to him too.

Mum came home unexpectedly early on Wednesday afternoon. She looked anxious.

'What's up?' Sam asked her.

Mum took a deep shuddery breath and said, 'Dr Robertson rang me at work. He wants you to go into hospital for some tests.'

Sam's heart shrank to a cold cinder.

'What kind of tests?' he said. 'Is something wrong?'

'Dr Robertson's not sure,' said Mum. 'He wants you to be examined by a specialist.'

Though he didn't feel much like joking, Sam said, 'Hey! I always told you I was special. That's why I need to see a specialist – it takes one to know one.'

Mum tried to smile and nearly brought it off. 'You'll have nurses running around after you all day,' she said. 'You'll be like a pig in muck.' Her attempted smile shrank. 'I'll come and visit you while you're in hospital.'

It seemed a strange thing to say.

'Cheers, Mum,' said Sam. 'I'll make sure I'm there for you to visit.'

The specialist was Dr Prosser, a tall Welshman in his fifties, with a frosting of white in his curly black hair, and a snaggletoothed grin. Sam thought that Dr Robertson had given him a pretty thorough examination, but Dr Prosser *really* put him through it. Sam was poked, prodded, jabbed, X-rayed, wired-up to monitors that beeped, and everything that went into and came out of his body was weighed and measured – which on a one-to-ten scale of embarrassment scored fifteen.

Dr Prosser met Sam and Mum on Friday afternoon, in an office on the first floor of the hospital. The office was small and quiet. Its single window looked out on to a brick wall. Dr Prosser sat behind a desk. Sam and Mum sat facing him, in tubular metal chairs with plastic backs and seats, just like the chairs in the main hall at school. There was a calendar pinned to the wall behind Dr Prosser. The picture on the calendar showed an old country house with lancet windows and tall chimneys.

Dr Prosser said, 'There are times when I don't like my job very much, and this is one of them. I don't believe in keeping the truth from my patients or their relatives, which is why I asked to see you together. There's no easy way for me to put this, so

I'll say it straight. Sam has Spengler's Syndrome.'

'I have *what*?' said Sam.

'Spengler's Syndrome,' Dr Prosser repeated. 'It's a condition that causes a progressive degeneration of the lymphatic system.'

'Can you give me the simple version?' Sam said.

'The lymphatic system carries oxygen and glucose to your cells, and carries away waste products, like carbon dioxide and urea. Unfortunately, your lymphatic system isn't working properly,' said Dr Prosser. 'As time goes on, your body will have increasing difficulty in feeding itself and the toxic waste products will build up. You'll experience the same symptoms that you're experiencing now – nausea, weakness and fainting – but they'll become more severe. I can prescribe some drugs that should ease your discomfort.'

Mum wriggled in her chair and said, 'Will Sam have to have surgery?'

'I'm sorry, Mrs Rawnsley,' said Dr Prosser, 'but at present there's no effective treatment available for Spengler's Syndrome. Patients may go into a remission that can last anything from a few months to three years, but the condition is' – he paused – 'invariably fatal.'

Sam thought, He didn't say that. I'm not here. I'm not me. He was talking about somebody else.

He was at war with his own body; the enemy he was fighting was himself.

Two

Sam went through disbelief, confusion, despair, terror and rage – and that was just for the first five minutes. After that he felt numb, as if his emotions had been given a hefty shot of sedative.

Mum didn't cry, but standing by the car in the hospital car park, she hugged Sam tightly.

'We're going to beat this!' she whispered. 'We'll find a way. I'm not going to let you go.'

Sam hugged her back, wishing that her determination could be contagious.

Over the weekend, Mum went into managerial mode, reorganizing everything she could think of. She planned out her workload so that she could spend more time at home, called relatives and friends and told them the news in a brisk, positive voice. Sam guessed that keeping herself busy was Mum's way of coping and let her get on with it, but they had a minor clash on Saturday afternoon when Mum said, 'I should ring your father.'

Sam's defences bristled like a porcupine's quills.

'What for?' he said.

'To let him know, of course.'

'What's it to him?'

Mum sighed. 'Be reasonable, Sam,' she said. 'He's your father. He has a right to know. He cares about you.'

'I don't want him involved,' Sam said stubbornly. 'He showed how much he cared about me they day he walked out. I don't like him and I don't like that little tart he's shacked up with.'

'Sam, you shouldn't—' Mum paused and reworded what she meant to say. 'It would hurt him if we kept it from him.'

Sam wasn't open to negotiation.

'Good,' he said. 'I want it to hurt him. He's earned it. He didn't seem to worry how much he hurt us, did he?'

Instead of replying, Mum plugged in her laptop, went online to check out every reference to Spengler's Syndrome that she could find, then made a list of the drugs that were used to treat it and what their side-effects were.

In contrast, Sam did his best to ignore Dr Prosser's diagnosis, treating it like a bad cut that he couldn't bring himself to look at, but at night the truth lunged at him from the darkness of his bedroom.

I'm going to die, he thought. *My life's going to come to an end. The world will carry on, but I won't be in it.*

He'd thought about death before, but only in a detached way. Death was inevitable, but it would come in the distant future and would happen to an old man. The old man would remember Sam as his young self, but would have a load of other memories that Sam didn't have, memories of the life that Sam hadn't yet lived – and now never would.

Sam recalled something that his mother had said when Grandad – her father – died. *He was ready to go.*

What does that mean? Sam thought. Ready for what, and to go where?

Bits of old RE lessons surfaced in his brain. There was plenty of choice, because almost every culture in the world believed in some kind of life after death. There were various sorts of paradise on offer, and reincarnation as well.

Hang on, though! Sam thought. Don't you come back because you've done something wrong and you have to do it over and over until you get it right?

He couldn't work out if reincarnation was a reward or a punishment, and he wasn't sure if he believed in an afterlife. He wasn't sure if he believed in God either, especially the kind of God who created a universe where Sam could develop Spengler's Syndrome.

Something he'd read somewhere came back to him, a poem or a story about a migrating swallow – or was it a sparrow? – flying at night, swooping in through the opened window of a room where a party was being held, then out through another open window into the blackness again. The bird caught a brief glimpse of light and colour, and people enjoying themselves, and that was life. The darkness on either side of the room stood for the

time before you were born, and for after you were dead.

Is that what death's like? Sam wondered. Night for ever, no moon and stars, no heat or cold, no wind or rain?

A huge shark of fear sank its teeth into his guts and shook him.

He needed a focus, something that would give meaning to the life he had left, and he had to find it quickly.

Time was running out.

Sunday was good – comparatively. The drugs Mum had picked up from the chemist's on Friday began to kick in, and Sam managed to keep his breakfast and lunch down, but he couldn't settle to read anything and death cropped up in all the programmes on TV, even the sports programmes. Sam got bored with just sitting, and went into the kitchen to find Mum. She was gazing out of the window into the back garden, her face pale and blank, but when she heard Sam's footsteps behind her, she turned towards him and forced a smile.

'How are you feeling?' she asked.

'About the same as when you asked me fifteen minutes ago. I think I'll take a walk.'

Mum raised her eyebrows. 'A walk?'

'Yeah,' said Sam. 'You know – like go outside and put one foot in front of the other?'

'I don't think you should, Sam.'

'I do. I think I should go for a walk while I still can.'

Mum nibbled at her bottom lip and said, 'I don't think you should, because Sean's coming over.'

For a moment Sam was puzzled. How could Mum possibly know what his best friend was going to do? Then he twigged.

'You told him,' he said.

'I rang him yesterday morning, before you got up.'

'You had no business to!' Sam said angrily. 'He's *my* friend.'

'I know, and I'm sorry, but I thought he ought to know. I thought it would help if you—' Mum's voice almost cracked and she gulped to steady it. 'Talking to a friend might do some good.'

'Sure!' said Sam. 'Sean might go to the science labs tomorrow and discover a cure.'

'Don't hold out on people, Sam. Don't push them away.'

'I am not pushing people away!' Sam snapped.

But he was. He dreaded talking to Sean, because he didn't want to be reminded of everything he was going to leave behind.

Sam and Sean had been mates since Year Seven. They'd gone to different junior schools, but had ended up in the same form at the Comp. The first time Sam saw Sean – skinny, clumsy, dark-haired and brown-eyed – he'd known that they were going to be friends. When they finally got around to talking, they discovered that they had an amazing amount in common. Like Sam, Sean was hooked on fantasy fiction, loathed football and soap operas, loved sci-fi and horror movies. They'd swapped thoughts and worries, bounced ideas off each other and cracked jokes that no one else understood. They'd become close as a result, and Sean was like the brother Sam had never had.

Sean arrived just after three, and Mum left him

and Sam alone together in the front room. Sean didn't say anything at first. He stood and stared at Sam, as if he was trying to memorize Sam's face.

When the silence became uncomfortable, Sam said, 'Aren't you going to sit down?'

'I don't want you to die, Sam,' Sean said.

'Me neither, but it seems I don't have a choice. Sit down, will you, Sean? And quit looking at me like that, it's freaking me out.'

Sean sat in the armchair in the bay window.

'It's not fair,' he said. 'Why did it have to be you? There are plenty of crap people in the world who deserve to die more than you do.'

'Go figure.'

Sean was tensed up and his hands were trembling.

'Say it,' said Sam.

'Say what?'

'What it is that you've come to say.'

Sean blurted out, 'I love you, Sam.'

'*What?*'

'Not like going-to-bed-together-type love,' Sean explained, 'but I care about you. I don't know what I'll – I mean, how can I—? Dammit, Sam, I feel guilty!'

Sam sensed how much it had taken for Sean to admit his feelings, and how much he was suffering.

'What, because I'm dying and you're not? That's crazy, Sean. It isn't your fault.'

'I don't know what to do.'

'Live for us both,' said Sam. 'Remember the laughs we had. Don't remember me after I got sick.'

'I'm not going to forget about you!' Sean said fiercely.

'You don't have to forget about me, Sean. I'm still here.'

Sean just couldn't get his head around it. Death was for old people, soldiers in battle, or accident victims. It wasn't supposed to happen to people in Year Eleven: they had futures in front of them, futures in which they might achieve anything. He spilled out his bewilderment and resentment in a barely comprehensible tirade. When he started crying, Sam felt embarrassed.

'Hey!' Sam said. 'Take it easy, Sean. Don't get upset.'

Sean sniffed and rubbed his nose with the back of his hand. 'How can you be so calm?'

Sam shrugged. 'What would be the point in getting stressed?'

'Are you scared?'

'Yes, I'm very scared, but I'm working on it.'

Sean shook his head in admiration. 'You're being incredibly brave.'

'No,' Sam said with a laugh. 'Dying is all I have left. I want to do it the best way I can.'

It was weird how things had reversed. Mum had thought that talking to Sean would help Sam, but Sean was the one who had needed help.

After Sean had gone, Sam went up to his bedroom, took a sheet of paper from his English folder and drew up a list of the things he'd thought he might do one day.

I'll never sleep with a girl.

I'll never go to university.

I'll never have a career.

I'll never get married.

I'll never have children.

I'll never go round the world.

I'll never grow old.

I'll never own a car, or a house, or a dog.

He dropped his biro.

This is feeble, Sam, he told himself. This is stuff you can't do anything about. Be positive – what *can* you do?

He couldn't think of a single thing.

Three

School was totally out of the question. On good days, Sam didn't feel normal exactly, but he felt a whole lot better than on bad days, when he was so weak that he could hardly drag himself out of bed. Dr Robertson made house calls, took more blood samples and sent them off to Dr Prosser who had them analyzed. Sam's dosage was adjusted according to the results.

Sean was a regular visitor, calling in on his way home from school, and during lunch hours on the days when Mum was at work. Once – and only once – he brought Jade with him. Jade seemed as embarrassed about it as Sam was, and he could tell that Sean had talked her into it. It would've been nice if she'd come to see Sam because she wanted to and not because she felt sorry for him, but Sam figured that time was way too short to kid himself.

Some of Sam's other friends visited too, but their conversations were punctuated with long awkward silences, and Sam understood why. He was at war, in the no man's land between the living and the dead. If he'd been healthy, his friends would have joked with him and given him all the latest school goss. If he'd been dead, they would have talked about what a great guy he'd been.

But I'm neither, Sam thought. Not really alive, but not quite dead. Leaving the present, but not in the past yet.

Some of his medication made time fluctuate. Minutes would expand into hours, hours contract into seconds. Even though Mum had warned him that this was likely to happen, Sam found it disconcerting. He lost days at a stretch, and the line that separated dreaming from reality became blurred. His dreams were so vivid that he preferred dreaming to being awake – he wasn't ill in the dream world – except when he dreamed about his father, which was more often than he would have liked.

One dream wove itself from memories of a summer trip to Cornwall. Sam and Dad were walking along a beach, looking across at St Michael's Mount. It was late afternoon and the weather was perfect. The castle hunched on its rock, the reflection of the sky in the calm sea and the family of swans swimming in the bay were like an illustration from a book about King Arthur.

Dad was the way Sam remembered him from childhood – big, funny, impulsive, more like an enlarged kid than a proper grown-up. They found flat pebbles in the sand and skimmed them over the surface of the water.

Dad said, 'What's the difference between a sick animal and a dead bee?'

'I don't know,' said Sam.

'One is a seedy beast, and the other is a bee deceased.'

The joke was so corny that Sam laughed at it.

'I'd die for you if I could, Sam,' Dad said. 'Parents shouldn't outlive their children. It's unnatural.'

Sam said, 'I don't want anyone to die. I want everybody to live for ever.'

He woke in tears.

'Dumb dream!' he whispered to the bedroom ceiling. 'Dumb, dumb dumb!'

The first time Sam heard his mother weep, it really tore him up. It happened late one night, long after he should have been asleep. Sam heard a hard, grudging sobbing, the sobbing of someone who'd fought giving in to misery, but had come to the end of their ability to hold out against it. Sam lay still in the dark, feeling helpless. If he went to comfort her, he'd be intruding on something he was sure that Mum wanted to keep private.

I'm doing that to her, Sam thought. She's crying over me.

To block out the sound of sobbing, Sam pictured his funeral. It was a little hazy – he hadn't made up his mind whether he'd be buried or cremated – but some of the details were clear.

Mum was there, with Aunt Pat and her husband Tony. Pat was Mum's big sister and gave her plenty of support, holding her arm around Mum's shoulders until the ceremony was over.

Dad was there too, despite all Sam's efforts to fade him out of the scene. Dad looked tired and drawn, and Sam hoped that he was regretting the wasted time when they could have been together. There were a few other members of Sam's family present, and behind them stood Sean, a couple of friends and Sam's form tutor, Mrs Ellis.

Sam didn't want a religious service, but there had to be music. Some of the techno stuff that he liked might be a bit too out there, but the last part of Beethoven's 6th Symphony ought to be right – the simple melody that was like a hymn.

And afterwards?

Sam hoped it wouldn't be like Grandad's funeral. The wake had been held in Grandad's house. Grandad's old cronies from the bowling club had stood around with glasses of beer or sweet sherry, shooting one another sideways glances, wondering whose funeral would be next. Sam had been fond of Grandad, but to hear Grandad's friends talk about him, you'd think that Grandad had been a saint.

I want people to remember who I really am, thought Sam.

And who was that? It was another thing that Sam had to work out in a hurry.

Sam was walking along the embankment of a river in a big city, through a fog so thick that he could hardly see from one lamppost to the next. The fog muffled the sound of traffic and shrank the world to the circle of Sam's vision. Though the city seemed familiar, he wasn't sure where he was – or who he was, or when it was. He approached the edge of the embankment to search for clues and found nothing but the fog and black, lapping water.

'You can never see it all,' said a voice.

Sam turned. Two or three metres away, a man was seated on a bench. He was plump, with silver hair and large eyes that bulged behind the wire frames of his spectacles. His black leather jacket was well-worn.

'See all of what?' asked Sam.

'What you're looking for,' said the man. 'When the war comes, many young men like you will think that it's what they were looking for.'

Thinking that the man was deranged and therefore

best humoured, Sam said, 'And *is* there going to be a war?'

'Don't be ridiculous!' the man said with a sniff. 'You've seen the future.'

Sam walked slowly over to the bench and sat down. 'Or is it the past?' he wondered aloud.

'That depends on which life you're in.'

'I have more than one life?' said Sam.

Close to, the man looked older. His face was as seamed and creased as his jacket. 'No,' he said. 'Only one life, but in many different forms. A raindrop, a stream and an ocean are all water, aren't they?'

'What does that have to do with anything?'

The man shrugged. 'It's not something that I can explain. You have to live it to understand.'

'I'm dying,' said Sam.

'Who isn't?' the man said.

Sam laughed. 'I must have popped one pill too many. You're not real, are you? You're a hallucination.'

'If you like,' said the man. 'If that makes it easier.' He put his hand inside his coat and—

'Sam?' said Mum, gently shaking Sam's shoulder. 'Sam, wake up. Sean's here.'

Sam was reluctant to leave the embankment, but he opened his eyes and let the real world return. His neck was stiff and his mouth tasted like the inside of a discarded trainer.

'Shall I make you both a cup of tea?' Mum asked.

'Please,' Sam mumbled.

Sean sat in his usual chair. Light from the bay window backlit his hair, turning it into a glowing auburn halo.

A dark angel, Sam thought.

'How's today been?' asked Sean.

'Sleepy,' said Sam. 'Sean, what am I like?'

'Like?'

'When other people look at me, what do they see?'

Sean puzzled for a moment.

'I'm not looking to have my ego boosted,' Sam said. 'Tell me like it is.'

Sean scratched his head. 'You're someone it pays to stay on the right side of,' he said. 'You can think of a put-down or a bad joke faster than anyone else I've ever met. You're the guy who can put what everybody's thinking into words. That puts some people off. They worry what you might say about them. Plus, of course, you're different.'

Sam laughed. 'Different as in weirdo loser, huh?'

'No, different as in special. I've been waiting for you to do something.'

'Such as?'

Sean shrugged. 'I don't know, write a book, make a movie, paint – something extraordinary.'

'It may be a little late for any of that,' Sam pointed out. 'And I don't have the energy. These days, what I mostly do is dream.'

'Maybe you should write your dreams down.'

Sam saw himself writing at a table made from a wooden crate, by the light of a candle in a wax-encrusted bottle. The book he was writing in had covers marbled in blue, black and white. His pen was a short wooden rod tipped with a steel nib, and what-ever he was writing was obviously flowing, because he frequently dipped the pen into a white inkwell. The walls around him were—

'Are you OK, Sam?' Sean said anxiously.

'Fine,' said Sam. 'I was just thinking, that's all.'

The sound of the key turning the lock on the front

door startled Sam back into time. He looked around at the front room, knowing where he was but not when. His last clear memory was talking to Sean about writing. Everything between then and now was a dark void.

Mum came into the room, looking pleased with herself.

'I've got some good news,' she said.

'Mum,' said Sam, 'what day is it?'

'Tuesday – why?'

'I just wondered. What's the good news?'

'We're going on holiday,' Mum said. 'John Fuller at work lets out a cottage on the Thames, and I've booked it for next week. We both need a break. Travelling abroad would be too tiring for you, but we can drive to the cottage in less than two hours. A change of scene would do us good.'

Mum meant that a change of scene would do her good, and she was right.

So, thought Sam. A cottage on the Thames – yeah, why not?

One of the advantages of dying was that you could do it anywhere.

Four

Sam and his mother left home on Friday evening and drove west on the M4 in heavy traffic. Many of the fantasy books that Sam had read had begun with a band of travellers journeying westwards on a quest. Now he was going west, but if he was on a quest, he didn't know what its goal was.

West, he thought. Sunsets, America and the Isles of Eternal Youth.

The car was moving fast but appeared slow. Other vehicles overtook at five miles an hour; lorries on the road ahead that were doing the same speed looked stationary. The smooth motion of the car lulled Sam into a series of micro-sleeps.

* * *

The month on the calendar in the hospital office had changed, but the picture of the country house was the same. Dr Prosser was wearing a uniform jacket – khaki with brass buttons. He was seated behind the desk, holding a glass bottle. The bottle contained a clear liquid that glittered like starlight.

'It's a truly remarkable breakthrough,' Dr Prosser said. 'You're a lucky young man.'

'Where did it come from?' Sam enquired.

Dr Prosser pointed to his left.

'The Western Front,' he said. 'They've made some remarkable breakthroughs.'

Sam looked at the liquid in the bottle. The twinkling light it gave off was hypnotic.

'How much do I have to take, Dr Prosser?'

'That's the drawback,' said Dr Prosser. 'I can't prescribe a dosage. You'll have to estimate the correct amount yourself.' He looked straight into Sam's eyes. 'It won't work until you've found what you need.'

'How do I do that?'

'I don't know,' said Dr Prosser. 'It's up to you to—'

* * *

Mum said, 'Don't go to sleep on me, Sam. I need you to map-read after we leave the motorway.'

Sam rubbed his eyes and twisted around to take the road atlas from the back seat.

'Whereabouts are we going?' he said.

'John ran off a set of directions for me,' Mum said. 'It should be in a polythene folder just inside the cover.'

Sam found the folder and began to read the instructions.

DIRECTIONS TO BANKSIDE COTTAGE

M4 – Junction 12 (NB all mileages are taken from this junction)

* Take the dual carriageway signposted – Theale A4/Pangbourne A340

* At 0.2 miles continue straight on over roundabout signposted – Theale A4/Pangbourne A340

* At 1.2 miles take second left at roundabout onto single carriageway signposted – Newbury A41/Basingstoke A340

Sam laughed. 'Is John a really organized guy who keeps his desk neat and tidy?' he said.

'Yes,' said Mum, sounding surprised. 'How did you know?'

'Lucky guess,' said Sam.

They arrived at a quarter to eight. The cottage was at the end of a track whose uneven surface made the car bounce and lurch. Sam's first view of it was via the light from the headlamps – a squat, two-storey building of brick and weathered wooden beams, with a pantiled roof.

What, no thatch? thought Sam. No roses twining around the door?

There was a trim front garden though, with a tablecloth-sized lawn surrounded by straight rows of daffodils.

'Does John pop over every weekend to cut the grass with nail-scissors?' said Sam.

'No,' Mum said. 'He pays someone to look after the garden. What d'you think?'

'I think it's a cottage, but I don't see any river-bank for it to be beside.'

'I expect it'll be there in the morning,' said Mum.

A worrying thought suddenly struck Sam. 'Mum, the cottage does have a bathroom, doesn't it?'

'Yes.'

'Good! I didn't fancy traipsing into the under-growth with a loo roll and a trowel.'

Mum smiled and said, 'It also has a stereo system and a TV – terrestrial channels only, I'm afraid.'

Sam shrugged.

'I'm going to like it here,' said Mum. 'I can tell already. Listen.'

Sam listened. 'I don't hear anything.'

'Exactly, It's peaceful. No traffic, no police sirens. The nearest big town is eight miles away.'

Let's hope we don't get burgled, thought Sam, but he didn't say anything.

The cottage was dark as well as quiet. Mum had a lot of trouble opening the front door, and then she had to fumble on tiptoe to find the electricity mains switch. When the switch clicked, a light came on in a hallway that was narrow enough to be a passage. A movement caught Sam's eye and he glanced down.

'Oh, what?' he gasped.

There were about a dozen brown butterflies on the floor of the hall. At first Sam thought they were alive, but it was only the draught from the open door rustling their wings.

They must have hatched out and starved to death, he thought. How long do butterflies live anyway — a few days, a week? They didn't even have that long. They didn't stand a chance.

Tears blurred Sam's vision and he blinked them away.

'Poor things!' Mum cooed. 'Oh, the poor things!'

Sam knew that she was thinking the same thing about the butterflies that he was thinking. They were just like him, dead before they'd really started.

Mum found a dustpan and brush in the cupboard under the sink in the cramped kitchen. Sam swept up the butterflies, and though he did it carefully, their brittle wings crumbled. Afterwards, he couldn't bring himself to throw them into the dustbin outside the back door, so he scattered them beneath a bush. They'd decay there, and the minerals in them would be absorbed by the soil and help plants to grow. Sam wondered if that was where the idea of re-incarnation had come from.

The cottage seemed to have been built at a time when people were smaller. The doorways were just high enough for Sam to pass through without ducking, and the modern(ish) three-piece suite in the front room took up most of the available floor space. The cottage had been extensively redecorated, but the redecoration had obviously been done on the cheap. All the electrical goods had been manufactured by companies Sam had never heard of and he could practically see the SPECIAL OFFER signs that must once have been plastered over them. The walls had been emulsioned in varying shades of beige and there were attempts at designer chic here and there – grains of rice in a glass-fronted frame hanging in the kitchen, a copper kettle in front of the gas fire in the boarded-up hearth and acid-bathed doors throughout. Yet despite the modernization, there was something about the cottage that resisted the twenty-first century, as if it had memories that it was reluctant to part with.

It ought to have bare floors and oil lamps, Sam thought.

Sam's bedroom had a small window that looked on to the back garden, though it was too dark for him to see anything. As he unpacked his suitcase and hung up his clothes, his mind wandered.

How old is this place? A hundred years, a hundred and fifty?

Many different people must have lived out their lives in it. It was strangely comforting for him to know that, should he die there, it would be nothing new to the cottage.

Sam woke early. Rays of bright sunshine slanted in through the window. He heard birds singing outside, and a raucous quacking of ducks that sounded like laughter.

'Must have been a cracking joke,' Sam said to himself.

As he now did every morning, Sam took a cautious inventory of his body, asking it questions: How are you this morning? What's your day going to be like?

The response was unexpectedly positive. His head wasn't aching and didn't spin when he moved, his stomach wasn't about to hurl last night's supper over the bedspread and the sore ache in his armpits and sides had gone away. Sam felt better than he had for weeks.

Dr Prosser's voice spoke in his head. *'This is totally unprecedented! Your illness has completely . . .'*

Sam cut off the voice.

Don't get carried away, Sam, he thought. You're having an extra-specially good start to the day, that's all. This afternoon you'll probably feel crap.

Since he was uncertain how long his sense of well-being might last, Sam decided to make the best of it. He slid out of bed, went to the window and looked out.

The back garden was long and thin, lined with rose bushes, and there was a fruit tree in white blossom. The garden path ended at a gate set into a low stone wall. Beyond the gate, the ground sloped down to a wooden jetty with mooring posts, and a broad stretch of grey-green river. On the opposite bank, massive weeping willows trailed their leaves in the water. A coot swam in the river, pushing its head forwards and jerking its body along. Further down the river, ducks circled and bobbed. It was such a typical countryside scene that it was almost ridiculous, like an animated picture postcard, but Sam didn't laugh because an unexpected surge of nostalgia surged through him. He knew this place, knew it as well as he knew the neighbourhood streets at home. If he went down to the river and walked upstream, he'd come to a stile set into a wooden fence. He could see the stile clearly in his mind, knew how its wood felt to the touch, how rain made it slippery, the way it creaked as it took his weight. He must have climbed over it hundreds of times on his way to—

To where? thought Sam. How can I know so much when I haven't been here before?

Something pulled at him, as if a piece of iron inside him was being drawn by a magnet. He had to go exploring, and he'd better do it before Mum woke up and raised all kinds of objections.

Sam washed and dressed. Downstairs in the kitchen he scribbled Mum a note – *Gone out for a while. Won't be long. Don't worry.* – left it on the table, quietly unbolted the back door and went outside.

The sun was warm on his face and the air tasted great. Sam walked down the garden path and opened the gate, smiling as the hinges squeaked. It was a familiar sound, even though he hadn't heard it before.

He closed the gate behind him and turned right along the riverbank, following a footpath. The path skirted the edge of a meadow whose overgrown grass was thick with wild flowers. With every step, the pull inside Sam grew stronger. When he'd walked about sixty metres he halted abruptly, his heart bumping like a bicycle wheel rolling over an uneven road.

The fence wasn't quite the same as he'd imagined it – it was made of barbed wire stretched between wooden uprights – but the stile was there, its wood green with moss.

Sam felt an excitement that was close to fear and tried to calm himself.

So you went for a walk in the country and you found a stile – big deal! he thought. If you'd gone in the opposite direction you'd probably have found another. There's nothing special about that. Go back to the cottage before Mum reads the note and comes after you.

But a less sensible part of Sam knew that something remarkable had happened, and that if he turned back he'd be refusing an invitation, though he had no idea what he was being invited to.

He clambered over the stile and looked around. Nothing seemed particularly different. The grass was still long and green, the wild flowers were just as brightly coloured. It was only when he glanced to his left that he registered how the river had stopped moving. The reflections on its surface had been stilled in mid-waver. And then Sam noticed other things: a sparrow hanging motionless in mid air, its wings pressed flat against its body; a ladybird frozen on the tip of a blade of grass. Nothing moved anywhere, as if time had been put on hold. Sam looked at his watch and saw that the second-indicator wasn't blinking.

'Wake up, Sam!' he growled. 'You're dreaming.'

But he knew that it was more than a dream. It had to be another freaky side-effect of the drugs he was taking. If he ignored what was happening – or rather what *wasn't* happening – and kept on going, the effect would wear off and things would put themselves right. He continued his way along the path, spotted something in the river and stopped to take a look.

A model yacht had snagged in a thicket of rushes. The boat was wooden and beautifully made, with a varnished deck, a canvas sail and silk rigging. The portholes above the waterline were glazed and trimmed in brass. The name of the yacht was painted in flowing golden letters on the bows – *BOURNE*.

Expensive toy! Sam thought. Whoever's lost it can't be pleased.

He looked around for the yacht's owner, but there was no one in sight, nor was there a stick that he could use to hook the boat. Sam scratched his chin as he estimated distances. If he got down on his stomach and stretched as far as he could, he might just be able to grab the yacht without falling into the river. He lay down and reached out, willing his arms to grow longer. The tips of his fingers snagged in the yacht's brass safety rail and he pulled the vessel closer. Sam stood up with the yacht clutched to his chest.

The river was flowing again. A breeze ruffled his hair.

There you go, Sam thought. All back to normal. If you carry on a bit further, you might find the person this boat belongs to. You can give it back to them and do your good deed for the day.

He entered the cool gloom of the clump of oak trees and stopped again. Someone was watching him; he could feel their eyes.

'Who's there?' he called out.

'I am, of course,' said an annoyed sounding voice. 'What kept you? I've been waiting an absolute age!' and a girl stepped out from behind a tree.

Five

She was thirteen or fourteen, Sam guessed, a girl but not a little girl. She had long light brown hair tied back in a black ribbon-bow, dark green eyes, a turned-up nose and a pointed chin. The bridge of her nose and her cheekbones were scattered with freckles. She was already striking and was going to be beautiful when she was older, but she'd have to change her taste in clothes. She wore a long-sleeved blouse with a pleated front and a high collar, and the hem of her navy blue skirt almost covered her black boots. It was an odd outfit for such a warm day and Sam wondered if she might be on her way to a fancy dress party, though it seemed a bit early for a party of any kind.

Then, with a shock, Sam realized that he was in fancy dress himself. Instead of a T-shirt, he was wearing an open-necked white shirt with rolled-back sleeves. His jeans had turned into a pair of linen trousers with a striped tie for a belt. The flip-flops he'd slipped on were now canvas shoes.

The girl glared at him and pouted. 'This is really too bad of you,' she said. 'You should have been here more than an hour ago. It's bad manners to keep a lady waiting.'

'I'm sorry,' said Sam, without being entirely sure why he was apologizing. 'I didn't know you were expecting me.'

'Then why are you carrying my boat?' the girl asked.

'Is this yours? I found it in the river just now.'

'Well of course you found it!' snapped the girl. 'I left it there for you.'

'You did?'

'It's our secret sign.'

Sam frowned in bewilderment. 'We have a secret sign?'

'How stupid you are today,' growled the girl. 'We

agreed this weeks ago. I told you that I would leave the boat in the reeds as a signal.'

'A signal of what?'

'That it's safe for us to meet. You know what Papa thinks.'

'Er, I don't as a matter of fact,' said Sam. 'Maybe you should explain.'

The girl's annoyance abruptly melted into a knowing smile. 'Ah, I see!' she murmured. 'In today's game we have never met before. You are a complete stranger.'

'That'd be right,' said Sam.

The girl turned her head and looked away. 'In that case, I couldn't possibly talk to you because we haven't been properly introduced.'

Sam said, 'That's easily fixed. I'm Sam Rawnsley.' He held out his right hand.

The girl regarded the hand as though it were something she'd found stuck on the sole of her boot after a long walk in the country. 'I don't know how people behave in your part of the country, Mr Rawnsley, but here a gentleman does not shake hands with a young lady,' she said. 'I'm sure I'm very pleased to make your acquaintance.'

Sam decided to enter the spirit of the girl's game and said, 'Likewise, Miss – er?'

'Marion Freelong,' said the girl. 'Are you a visitor to the area, Mr Rawnsley?'

'On holiday,' Sam said. 'My mother and I are staying at Bankside Cottage. She rented it from this guy she works with.'

'Your mother works?' said Marion, raising an eyebrow. 'How contemporary! In what sort of work is your mother engaged?'

'She's a software designer.'

Marion blinked rapidly. 'I don't recall having heard that term before,' she said, 'but please don't bother to explain, it's bound to be tedious. Work is always tedious, is it not? What of you, Mr Rawnsley, how are you currently employed?'

'I'm not,' said Sam. 'I'm still at school.'

'And after you leave school – have you any particular career in mind?'

'I haven't really given it much thought.'

'But you should,' Marion chided. 'One should always have an object, otherwise one simply drifts aimlessly through life. I intend to be an actress, or a writer, or marry a rich man and travel the world.'

'That's got just about all your bases covered,' Sam joked.

Marion tutted. 'Really, Mr Rawnsley, your speech is so outlandish that I can hardly understand the half of what you say.'

Sam smiled. 'Hey, you're really good at this, aren't you?' he said. 'You talk like someone out of a Victorian novel.'

'And that meets with your disapproval?'

'No. Actually it's sort of cute.'

'Cute or not, Mr Rawnsley, let me assure you that I am very much a young woman of the twentieth century,' said Marion. 'Papa considers some of my views extremely radical.'

'Twenty-*first* century,' said Sam, correcting her.

Marion's eyes turned as cold as marble. 'I beg your pardon, Mr Rawnsley, but I am fully aware in which century I'm living.'

A possibility that explained Marion's old-fashioned clothes and way of talking occurred to Sam and he felt a chilly prickling at the back of his neck. 'Are you a ghost?' he whispered.

Marion laughed delightedly. 'Why, I'm as much a ghost as you are!' she declared.

'And how much of a ghost is that?' said Sam.

'I'm sorry, Mr Rawnsley, but I make a point of never gratifying impertinent questions,' Marion said, then her face relaxed. 'Oh, Sam, you are priceless, you know. If it weren't for these games of ours, I should be bored to tears – or to death.'

The tenderness in Marion's voice released something in Sam's head. He had intense flashes of memories that weren't his. Places he hadn't been and faces he hadn't seen before zipped through his brain like a video on fast-forward. When the flashes stopped he was still Sam, but not the same Sam that he'd been before. He found himself saying, 'Your father thinks that now we're older, we shouldn't meet without a chaperone. That's what the secret sign stuff is about, isn't it?'

Marion nodded. 'What Papa thinks is all my eye!' she said. 'If a chaperone were with us, we shouldn't be able to talk like this, should we? We should have to talk about the weather, or the horse and flower show, or all the other meaningless drivel that makes up polite conversation, and I'd hate that.'

'So would I,' said Sam.

Marion hesitated for a moment, then said softly, 'Shall I tell you a secret that I haven't told to anyone?'

'If you think you can trust me with it.'

'I know I can,' said Marion. 'I sometimes feel that the only time I'm real is when I'm with you, and that everything else is a dream. Does that seem silly to you?'

'No,' said Sam. 'That's my secret too.'

Marion flicked out of existence like a failed light bulb and the toy boat vanished from under Sam's left arm. A wood pigeon flew out of one of the oak trees, startling Sam with the clatter of its wings. He was wearing the clothes that he'd put on in the cottage. When he consulted his watch, he found that he'd been out walking for less than ten minutes.

I've cracked, he thought. I'm insane.

But did insane people know they were insane, or did they think that they were normal and everyone else was crazy? It had to be the drugs, fuelling a fantasy so strong that Sam felt as if he could step into it and lose himself. It had already provided him with clothes, false memories and Marion Freelong – especially Marion Freelong.

Mum was in the kitchen when Sam got back, slotting sliced bread into a toaster. Beside the toaster, an electric kettle wheezed and clicked as it came to the boil.

'You can have toast or toast for breakfast,' Mum said. 'I'll find a supermarket later. John says you can get a good deal on eggs from the local farmers. Did you enjoy your walk?'

'Kind of,' said Sam. 'I met this really strange girl.'

'What was strange about her?'

Sam decided to give Mum a carefully edited version of the truth – whatever that was. 'Her name's Marion,' he said. 'She lets her imagination run away with her. She talked to me about all kinds of weird stuff.'

The kettle boiled. Mum turned it off at the plug. 'It sounds as if the natives are friendly anyway,' she said.

'I don't know about friendly, but if Marion's

anything to go by, they're certainly different,' said Sam.

I sometimes feel that the only time I'm real is when I'm with you, and that everything else is a dream, he thought, and with the memory came a hunch that he hadn't seen the last of Marion Freelong. Drug-induced hallucination or not, they had unfinished business.

Six

Just as Sam had feared, on Saturday afternoon his symptoms came back with a vengeance. It happened when he was helping Mum to unload the shopping from the car, and began with a sharp dirty headache that sent a skein of bright dots swarming across his field of vision. Shortly after he was struck by a high tide of nausea and spent ten minutes with his head down the loo, vomiting until his stomach muscles were sore.

Sam hated it when his body went out of control, and he was all illness and no him. He waited until he got his breath back, then stood up, worked the flush, washed his face and brushed his teeth. He felt as if he'd been given a good kicking by a rugby team.

Mum was waiting outside the bathroom, trying to hide the worry in her eyes. She handed Sam a glass of water and a fat grey-white tablet. Sam recognized the tablet as a dose of the strongest drug that he'd been prescribed.

'Not that stuff again!' he groaned. 'It knocks me cold.'

'Take it,' said Mum.

'I'll be all right in a sec.'

'Sam,' said Mum, 'please don't argue.'

Sam reluctantly swallowed the tablet and went to lie down.

He dreamed and dreamed and dreamed.

He was walking across a field in warm sunshine. Beside him was the man he had met on an embankment in a dream. Sam didn't feel surprised that the man was there, nor that they were both wearing army uniforms. A holstered pistol hung heavily against Sam's hip.

The field was lush and green, but the going was uneven. Sam and the man stumbled through ruts and potholes, clambered over banks.

'What place is this?' said Sam.

'This was a section of no man's land,' the man said. 'Armies died trying to take and hold it, but none succeeded. No man's land belongs to no one and no one belongs to it. It's outside time, a step on a journey between one thing and another.'

Sam stopped walking and looked around at the bright splashes of flowers among the grass. At the far end of the field, a rabbit broke cover with a white flash of tail.

'It's peaceful here,' he said.

'The peace was bought with thousands of lives,' said the man. 'Some who died were prepared for it, some were not. Death took them anyway, the brave with the cowardly, the clever with the stupid.'

'It doesn't make sense!' Sam murmured.

'It doesn't have to make sense,' said the man. 'The troops died, the future followed and no one knows whether that future was better or worse for what happened here. This is where the soldiers found their real selves, their courage – or lack of it – their strengths and weaknesses.'

'Is that why you brought me here, to think about death and find my real self?'

The man laughed like a barking dog. 'You're the one who brought you here, Sam,' he said. 'I'm only—'

Sam opened his eyes. It was light. The drug held him in deceptive comfort, cocooning him in thick duvets that separated him from the chaos in his body. He felt rumours of pain, but not pain itself. The travelling alarm-clock on the bedside table told him that he'd been asleep for two hours.

Drowsiness plucked at him like undertow. His unfinished dream wanted an ending, but Sam fought hard against returning to the field. He concentrated on Marion Freelong, using her memory as a lifebelt to keep him afloat in consciousness.

He saw her eyes, her hair, the way the tip of her nose moved when she talked. She was totally unlike his usual fantasy girls, who tended to be on the passive side, and when he'd talked to her, he hadn't been calling the shots as he did in daydreams he'd had about Jade. Marion was mysterious and feisty.

Why her? Sam thought. She's not a princess in distress. She doesn't live in a castle guarded by a minotaur. I've never fantasized about anybody like her before.

But he had now, and there had to be a reason for it.

Sam tried to make Marion appear in the room, but she wouldn't be conjured.

Interesting, he mused. This is my fantasy, but I don't control it. I've created a female character who doesn't do what her author says.

Gradually – so gradually that it didn't register – Sam's intrigue became fascination.

At five o' clock, he felt strong enough to get up. He went downstairs, taking it easy, so that his feet would go where they were supposed to. The drug was wearing off, leaving his head feeling as though it had been packed with cotton wool.

Mum was in the front room, using her laptop. She'd plugged the computer into a nearby phone socket. When Sam came in, Mum looked up from the screen.

'Feeling better?' she said.

'A bit.'

'Would you like something to eat?'

Sam's stomach turned a figure of eight. 'Not at the moment,' he said then added, knowing that Mum would say it if he didn't, 'I guess I ought to eat something, though. Maybe I'll have a bowl of soup later. What are you doing?'

'Just catching up with some work.'

The computer chimed and a smooth female voice emerged from the speakers: *You've got mail!*

Mum shut the laptop's lid.

'Aren't you going to open the message?' said Sam.

'It can wait.'

Mum unplugged the computer and reconnected the phone.

She was obviously hiding something from him, and if Sam had been feeling better he might have become angry about it, but he let it go. He sat down and ran a hand through his hair.

'That drug gives me nightmares,' he said.

'You've always had nightmares,' said Mum. 'When you were a small child, you used to sleepwalk.'

This was news to Sam.

'I did?' he said. 'Where did I go?'

'Onto the landing. You drew on the wall with your finger.'

'What did I draw?'

'I don't know,' said Mum. 'Your father wanted to give you a crayon, but then we thought about how much it would cost to redecorate.'

'How come you never told me before?'

'You grew out of it,' Mum said with a shrug. 'It was just a phase you went through.'

Except perhaps it wasn't a phase, Sam thought. What if the thing that made me sleepwalk evolved, changed direction, made me see things when I was awake, as well as asleep?

Imagination was something that everybody had, more or less, and so everybody took it for granted, but the more Sam thought about it, the more extraordinary imagination seemed. It could take you anywhere, to places that would never exist.

Sam wanted to find out more about what was in his imagination – particularly the part of it that had invented Marion Freelong.

* * *

The dream was familiar – an old favourite – and the Sam in the dream knew that he was dreaming. He was hurrying along a street, late for school. His shirt had a grimy collar, its top button was missing and he wasn't wearing his uniform tie. He'd forgotten all his books, and what lesson he should be going to. Added to which, when he got to school everything had been rearranged. A staircase that should have taken him up to the History department led him to the sports hall, which was also a library, with tall bookcases standing where the wall bars had been.

Sam left the sports hall and found himself in a corridor that linked the top floors of two teaching blocks. Half way down the corridor was a room that contained a writing desk and a chair. Sam went into the room and sat at the desk. Laid out in front of him were a dip-in pen, a white inkwell and a large book with a cover marbled in blue, black and white. Sam opened the book, charged the pen with ink and wrote, *Sam woke up*.

And Sam woke up.

A ray of moonlight shone through a gap in the curtains and slanted across the bedroom. Within the ray, motes of dust hung motionless. Sam listened for the ticking of his alarm clock, but it was silent – everything was silent.

He swung out of bed, put on his slippers and dressing gown, went downstairs and out into the back garden. The roses looked black in the moonlight. The blossom on the fruit tree glowed silvery-white, and the trunk of the tree was grey. As he walked down the garden path, Sam noticed that the jetty seemed longer, and that someone was standing near a boathouse at its far end – a young woman with her back turned to him. She wore a long white satin dress trimmed with lace. Her hair, glossy in the light of the moon, almost reached her waist.

Marion? Sam thought.

But no, it couldn't be Marion. Marion was smaller and thinner.

The young woman gave no sign of hearing Sam, and didn't move when the hinges of the gate squeaked. He stepped onto the jetty, a board creaked and the young woman looked over her shoulder. Either Marion had a big sister, or she'd grown older. The same freckles were on her face, but her features had settled into a loveliness that made Sam stand still inside.

'Marion?' he said, and as he spoke her name, memories crowded in, filling the gap of the missing years. She was seventeen now and he was twenty. The misunderstandings, rows and reconciliations they'd been through had made their friendship deepen.

'You knew that you would find me here, didn't you?' said Marion. 'I always seek the comfort of the river when I'm troubled.'

Once again Sam found himself using the kind of words that Marion used, but this time they came to him easily. The only thing about this that surprised him was that he wasn't surprised. 'What's troubling you?' he said.

'You are. How could you do it, Sam? How could you dance with Rosie Fisher that way?'

Now that Marion had come to mention it, Sam noticed that he was dressed for dancing. He was wearing a dinner suit and the stiff collar of his shirt was chafing his neck. He remembered how the chandeliers in the ballroom had sparkled as he'd whirled the warm armful of Rosie Fisher around the dance floor, and how Marion had rushed through the opened French windows into the night. Though he'd known that she'd been manipulating him, running off so that he'd come after her, he hadn't been able to resist.

'I only danced with her because your father asked me to,' Sam said. 'She hadn't danced all evening and he was concerned that she might be feeling left out.'

Marion's eyes flashed. 'You flirted with her!' she said. 'I saw the looks you gave each other.'

'I didn't flirt with her. Rosie Fisher means nothing to me.'

'She appeared to mean something to you while you were dancing.'

'Then appearances can be deceptive.'

Marion stamped her foot, exactly as she had when she was a little girl, and her shoe clunked against the planking of the jetty. 'Couldn't you see what Papa was doing?' she said angrily. 'He tricked you into dancing with Rosie in the hope that you would like her more than you like me.'

'I'm afraid I'll have to disappoint him there,' said

Sam. 'I hardly know the girl. How can I possibly like her more than I like you?'

'Aha! So you admit that you *do* like her?'

'She's pleasant enough, I suppose but—' Sam broke off with an exasperated sigh. 'Are you seriously jealous, Marion, or is this another game?'

The corners of Marion's mouth twitched. Sam couldn't tell if she were about to smile or burst into tears.

'That is for me to know and you to find out,' Marion said.

Sam's right hand moved automatically to his jacket pocket for his cigarette case and matches. He took out a cigarette, tapped it against the lid of the case to tamp down the tobacco and lit it. He felt more at home in the fantasy this time, and Marion's style of speech came easily to him.

Marion scowled. 'I do wish you hadn't taken up smoking, Sam, and I wish you hadn't grown that ridiculous moustache.'

Sam raised his left hand and stroked the hair on his upper lip. 'Don't you think it makes me look distinguished?'

'No, it makes you look like a little boy playing let's pretend.'

'Isn't that what we're both doing?'

Marion made no reply.

'Anyway, what if I did like Rosie Fisher more than I like you,' Sam teased. 'Would you mind that much?'

'You know I would.'

'Do I?'

Marion gazed at the moonlight on the surface of the river. 'When we were children, you swore that we should always be sweethearts,' she said. 'I believed that you meant it.'

'And so I did – when I was a child,' said Sam, 'but there comes a time when childish things have to be left behind.'

'Be careful what you say, Sam,' Marion warned. 'You can make a thing come true by saying it. It's a powerful gift that you should use wisely.'

Sam wasn't certain what Marion meant. 'What is this?' he said, 'When we're together, where am I?'

'With me,' said Marion.

'But are you real, or am I imagining you?'

'Or is it I who am imagining you?' Marion said.

And she wasn't there. The jetty was short again and Sam was in his dressing gown and slippers. He stared at the spot where Marion had stood, wishing that she hadn't gone and already longing to see her again. With the longing came a feeling that he recognized. He was in love with her, or falling in love.

Maybe she's a witch, Sam thought. Maybe she uses a magic spell to pull me out of time and— No, Sam. You read that in *The Lair of the Golden Dragon*. You have to make up your own plot.

He walked slowly back to the cottage, wondering where he would take the story, or where the story would take him.

Seven

Sunday morning started off bright but quickly turned sullen. The air was thick and damp, with an unbroken thunderstorm in every breath. When they finished breakfast, Sam and Mum went for a drive to look for a Sunday newspaper. They stopped in a village a few kilometres from the cottage, and while Mum went into a newsagents, Sam took a stroll along the main street. It didn't take him long – a mini-market-cum-post office, a pub, a terrace of houses, a church and that was it. Inside the church, an out-of-tune piano played, and what sounded like a thin congregation raised its voices in a hymn. The effect was sad and slightly eerie.

Outside the church was a war memorial, a

rough-hewn stone cross inscribed, *In loving memory of those who laid down their lives in the Great War 1914–1918*. The inscription was followed by a list of names – some strangely familiar, like Batt, Gray and Foxton – and the ages the soldiers had been when they were killed. There were thirty names in all, and some of the men hadn't been much older than Sam.

In a little village like this, that kind of loss must have been devastating, Sam thought.

The singing in the church stopped and Sam felt time stop with it. The cross disappeared and the street changed, lost the modern facades on the shops and the TV aerials on the roofs of the houses.

Soldiers in khaki uniform came down the street, marching four abreast with packs on their backs and rifles at their shoulders. A Jack Russell terrier pranced beside them, yapping excitedly. The pavements were lined with people cheering and waving. Sam looked for Marion in the crowd, but he couldn't see her.

The soldiers' boots raised a rolling cloud of dust that enveloped the men at the rear, but they didn't break step, or cough, or rub their eyes. They looked straight ahead, their mouths set in determined lines. The expressions on their faces suggested that the war was as good as won. They hadn't seen the monuments, or observed the two minutes' silence on Remembrance Day. All of that lay in the future – for those who had a future. Those who didn't would be slaughtered on the battlefields of Northern France and Belgium, watching their lives bleed away into the mud, or having their bodies shredded by shrapnel. Sam identified with the ones who wouldn't be coming back because they were doomed to an early death, as he was.

Is that why I can see them? he thought. Does what we have in common make a bridge through time? In a strange sort of way, he even envied the men. They believed that they were taking part in a war that would end all wars, and the fact that it hadn't ended all wars didn't weaken the strength of their convictions, or make their hopes less admirable.

The soldiers rounded a corner and the present shifted. Sam turned and walked to the car.

Mum came out of the newsagents a minute or so later. 'Boy, the woman behind the counter in there can certainly talk!' she said. 'Pop in to buy a paper and you end up listening to the story of her life. She even showed me pictures of her grandchildren.'

Sam felt it strike Mum that she'd never have the chance to show off pictures of her own grandchildren, because there weren't going to be any.

'Nice kids?' he said.

'Very nice, but the way their grandmother rattles on, it's a wonder they've got any ears left.'

Mum was quiet during the return drive. Sam suspected that she was finding the holiday a double-edged sword. Freedom from routine was giving her more time to think and more things to face.

Back at the cottage, Mum and Sam carried chairs out onto the lawn and sat in the sun. Boats passed along the river. A family on a hired barge waved as they passed by. Sam made a show of reading the paper, but his head was full of Marion. He wanted to be with her so badly that it hurt. He'd never known a girl like her before. She was so easy to talk to, far easier than Jade, who made him tongue-tied.

Sam had been out with a few girls, but the dates hadn't been successful because they never went as well as he imagined they would beforehand. His imaginary dates had been shot in soft focus, with romantic music on the soundtrack. The reality of going to a club or a movie didn't compare. In reality, girls didn't instantly understand him on a level that went beyond words, he had to make conversation with them, and small talk wasn't Sam's strong suit. He went quiet and shy, and girls thought he was being distant and offhand. After a particularly disastrous evening, one girl had said, 'Why did you ask me out when you don't like me?' And Sam had been too embarrassed to answer. The truth was that he cared too much. The cliché that males were only interested in one thing and girls wanted commitment didn't apply to Sam. He wanted a relationship, wanted to know what it felt like to love someone who loved him back.

'I hope this isn't too boring for you,' Mum said.

'I'm not bored, just relaxed,' said Sam. 'Mum, why did you and Dad split up?'

Mum stiffened, then turned a page of the paper so smartly that it ripped.

'What brought that on?' she said. 'I told you all about it at the time.'

'No you didn't,' said Sam. 'You talked a lot of guff about how the divorce didn't mean that you and Dad had stopped loving me. Anyway, I wasn't really listening because I was too angry. So what happened?'

Mum gazed into the middle distance.

'We outgrew each other,' she said at last. 'We stopped having fun together. Your father didn't like the amount of time my career took up, or the fact that I earned more than he did.'

'A woman's place is in the home, huh?' Sam commented.

'That and a lot of other things.'

'Like the affair he had with a member of his staff?' said Sam.

'She was a symptom, not a cause,' Mum said. 'Your father and I drifted further and further apart, until in the end we were like strangers.'

'And what about love?'

Mum smiled sadly. 'We were in love at the start, but we changed from the people we were then,' she said. 'A part of me is still in love with the crazy English student who was going to write the finest novel of his generation.'

Sam couldn't believe it. 'Dad wanted to be a writer?'

'That's why he went into teaching. He thought he'd be able to write in the holidays, but what he mostly did was marking and lesson preparation. Then you were born, and neither of us had any time for anything but surviving.'

Writing, thought Sam. Is my imagination a genetic thing – did I inherit it from Dad?

He didn't like the idea. He didn't want to have anything in common with his father.

In the afternoon, Sam borrowed Mum's laptop and sent an e-mail to Sean, and didn't realize that he'd fallen asleep until the sound of a voice calling his name woke him up. He surfaced, blinking. There was drool on his chin and he wiped it away. The laptop's monitor showed a screen-saver, the logo of the company Mum worked for. Sam yawned and frowned. Something in the atmosphere of the room had changed. The air was charged with static and expectancy.

Sam swivelled round and saw his father standing

behind him. There were bright streaks on Dad's face – tears reflecting the light from the window.

'What do you want?' Sam demanded.

'To see you,' said Dad.

'Yeah? Well now you have, mind the door doesn't hit you on the butt as you leave.'

Dad looked a mess. There was stubble on his chin and puffy bags under his eyes. He seemed to have aged about ten years since the last time Sam saw him.

Dad said, 'Your mother and I have been e-mailing each other. I had to come, Sam.'

'Why?'

Dad began to raise his arms, then let them drop to his sides. 'I'm your father,' he said.

'Only biologically,' said Sam. 'You gave up on the rest three years ago.'

Dad flinched and said, 'Don't, Sam. It took me four hours to drive here.'

'Really?' said Sam. 'How was the traffic?'

He was appalled at how easy it was to hurt his father, and how satisfying it felt.

Dad said, 'D'you really hate me that much?'

Sam recognized Dad's tone. It was his Mr Rawnsley voice, the one he used to lay guilt-trips on uncooperative pupils.

'I don't anything you, Dad. I gave up on you, like you gave up on me.'

'I was hoping that one day you'd get over your resentment and find some room for me in your life, but—' Dad swallowed hard. 'I'm afraid, Sam, afraid of what's happening to you and afraid of how I'll react.'

Sam was taken aback. He'd expected remorse from his father, but not fear. Once again, as in his conversation with Sean, Sam saw that dying wasn't a problem, but mourning was.

'Don't be scared, Dad,' he said. 'There's nothing to be scared of.'

'I know I made a mess of my marriage, Sam, but I didn't mean to hurt you. You were an innocent bystander who got caught in the crossfire. I'm not sorry for what I did, but I'm sorry for the way I did it. Can you forgive me?'

'No,' said Sam. 'I haven't got time to forgive anyone, Dad. You'll have to find a way of forgiving yourself. You made your choice and I had to live with it. Now you have to live with mine.'

'I tried to be a good father, Sam.'

This is an act, Sam thought. He's written himself a star role – the grieving father of a doomed son – for what, a deathbed reconciliation?

He said, 'I know you did, Dad, and you were pretty convincing most of the time. Hang on to that, and stop beating yourself up because I'm dying.'

Drowsiness rolled over Sam, like dark surf. The light in the room started to fade, and Dad faded with it.

Dad said, 'If you need me for anything—'

'OK,' said Sam, 'but don't hold your breath.'

The surf closed over his head.

He was watching TV in the front room. The phone rang and Mum went to answer it.

She said, 'Yes. Yes. Yes,' then, 'What?' Mum came back into the room, all smiles. 'It's for you,' she said.

'Who is it?'

'Take the call and find out.'

Sam stumbled into the hall and lifted the receiver to his ear.

'Hello?' he said.

A female voice said, 'Is that Sam Rawnsley?'

'Yes.'

'This is Sister Hollier from St Margaret's Hospital. It seems we owe you an apology, Mr Rawnsley.'

'Oh?' said Sam.

'We're not sure how it happened, but there's been an unfortunate clerical error. Your blood sample was mixed up with the sample from another patient, and you were wrongly diagnosed.'

A firework of hope exploded inside Sam's chest.

'You mean I don't have Spengler's Syndrome?' he said.

'You have glandular fever, Mr Rawnsley . . .'

Mum tapped Sam on the shoulder and said, 'Sam?'

Sam opened his eyes. He was in the cottage, stretched out on the sofa that was too small for him. He couldn't recall how he'd got there.

Mum offered Sam a glass.

'I made some iced tea,' she said. 'I thought you might like some.'

'I talked to Dad,' he said.

Mum looked pleased and puzzled.

'Did he ring you?' she said.

'No, he was here.'

'When?'

'Earlier on. Didn't you see him? Don't tell me he sneaked off without talking to you.'

'Sam,' Mum said gently, 'your father can't have been here. I happen to know that he's attending a headmasters' conference in Edinburgh and won't be back until next Friday.'

So they've been in touch, thought Sam, but he didn't ask Mum about it.

He said, 'Oh. Must have been a dream. Probably just as well. The conversation went better than it would have in real life.'

'I wish you would ring him,' said Mum. 'I know the number of his hotel.'

Wish on! Sam thought.

Eight

Even with the bedroom window wide open and the covers turned back, Sam was too hot to sleep. The air was stifling and his pillow was damp with sweat. The humidity made thoughts flourish like mental bindweed in his brain. It was now almost impossible for Sam to distinguish what was a dream, what was a fantasy and what was real. The drugs that he took were keeping him alive, but what kind of life were they keeping him in?

And what's reality anyway? Sam thought. When I eat something I can taste it, smell it and touch it so I think it's real, but that's just my senses feeding data to my brain. Suppose my senses get things wrong, or my brain doesn't process the information properly? If I get a heavy cold, I can't smell flowers – does that mean they've lost their scent?

A low growl of thunder rippled in the distance. Hoping that it was going to rain soon, Sam rolled off the bed and crossed to the window. Boiling banks of dark cloud were massing, swallowing the stars. A cool breeze gusted in his face.

'Storm's on its way,' Sam whispered and as he said it, a jagged spark of lightning lit the room, like a flashbulb.

The first raindrops fell with a sizzling noise on the back lawn. The leaves of the fruit tree twitched. Black freckles appeared on the garden path. Then the rain intensified: white lances flew past the window; the gutters overhead chuckled and dripped. There was more thunder, louder this time, and a dazzling bolt of lightning that crackled.

An instinctive fear crawled up Sam's spine, but he smiled because he loved the way that thunderstorms made him feel small.

It suddenly dawned on Sam that he'd never taken a walk in the rain because he'd wanted to. He'd been caught in storms and soaked, but that hadn't been voluntary.

If you want to find out what it feels like, this could be your last chance, he thought.

In an ideal world, Sam would have gone naked into the rain, but if Mum woke up and saw him it would be more humiliation than he could handle, so he slipped on a T-shirt, jeans and a pair of flip-flops, and crept downstairs.

As Sam stepped over the threshold of the back door, he felt a twitch like the twitch he felt in a lift when his stomach told him that he was moving and his eyes told him that he was stationary.

The storm freeze-framed. The rain halted in the air, gleaming like Christmas decorations in the glare of a lightning bolt that was a crystal crack in the sky. Raindrops, stilled at the moment of their impact on the surface of a puddle, formed tiny liquid crowns.

Sam walked down the path, globules of water bursting against his clothes and skin. By the time he reached the gate, his T-shirt was drenched. Sam opened the gate and when he turned to close it, saw that he'd left a trail in the rain, a narrow corridor of empty air. The corridor collapsed as the storm recommenced. The lightning flicked out and was almost immediately followed by a roar of thunder.

Marion came along the riverbank path, holding up the hem of her long skirt so that she could run. She wore a dark hooded cloak, the hood raised to protect her from the weather. She flung herself at Sam, cupped his face in both her hands and kissed his cheeks, eyes and forehead, murmuring his name over and over. Her mouth found his and they kissed warmly in the cold rain. Sam held her tightly, so that nothing mattered – not the thunder, or the downpour, or sickness, or death – only the intensity of their closeness.

The kiss ended. Marion said, 'Let's shelter in the boathouse.'

They ran to the end of the jetty, holding hands. The boathouse door was slightly ajar. They went inside and Sam closed the door behind them. The dark interior was filled with the sound of the rain on the roof. Sam caught his breath, dazed by the new sensations the kiss had roused in him.

Marion's voice came out of the darkness. 'Do you remember that winter when we were ten and we went tobogganing in the snow on Beacon Hill, Sam?'

And he did remember: Marion in a heavy grey coat, with mittens on her hands and a tartan Tam o' Shanter cap on her head. They'd laughed until their sides hurt. Even then Sam had known he'd never meet anyone else like her.

'Yes,' he said.

'I didn't think I would ever be that happy and excited again,' said Marion. 'But I am now.'

'And I didn't know I could feel like this about anyone,' Sam said.

Marion squeezed his hand. 'We're lucky, you know, to have each other. I think it's rare for people to feel the way that we feel.'

'But it's not real!' Sam groaned.

Marion squeezed his hand harder. 'Does that seem real to you?'

'Yes.'

'Is our love real?'

'Yes.'

'Then nothing else matters.'

Sam, judging that the time was right for confessions, said, 'I wish it was that easy, but it's not. I'm dying. I have Spen—'

Marion placed her fingers on his lips to silence him. 'Don't, Sam!' she whispered. 'Everyone must die, but for you and I death is a gateway to something else. I know this is difficult for you to understand, but time is short and we must continue the game.' Her expression changed. She took her hand away from his face. 'Shall you go to Papa and seek his permission for our engagement?'

Sam had been right about confessions, but wrong about what it was that he had to confess. He wasn't ill in Marion's world, but there was still something that he'd delayed telling her until the last possible moment, and the last possible moment had arrived. 'Under the circumstances, I don't think that we should become engaged just yet,' he said.

'Under what circumstances?'

'The war.'

Marion was ahead of him. 'You have enlisted,' she said in a flat voice.

'I'm to be granted a commission as a lieutenant,'

said Sam. 'I leave for training camp at the end of the week.'

Marion gave a bitter laugh. 'You consider it your duty to fight for king and country, I suppose?' she said.

'Nothing as noble as that,' Sam admitted. 'I just can't idly stand by while others go off to war. It makes me feel guilty.'

'But what does that have to do with our engagement?'

'I don't want to hold you to a promise that you might come to regret later,' said Sam. 'Should I be crippled or killed, it would be better if you were free to find happiness with someone else.'

'If you were crippled, I should care for you,' Marion said. 'If you were killed, I should grieve. What use would my freedom be without you, Sam? There can be no one else for me but you. You are me, and I am you, and we cannot be ourselves without each other.'

The darkness of the boathouse became the darkness of the night. Sam was alone on the jetty, in the rain.

Nine

On Monday morning, Mum was up long before Sam. He heard her bustling about, moving furniture, opening and closing cupboard doors, and guessed that she was tidying up the cottage.

She must have reached the point where relaxation changes into boredom, Sam thought, and he turned out to be right, because when he went downstairs Mum was on the sofa in the front room, sipping coffee as she consulted a road atlas and a National Trust guide book.

'Sleep well?' she asked.

'So-so,' said Sam. 'The thunderstorm kept me awake for a while.'

'There was a thunderstorm? I didn't hear a thing. I slept like a baby.'

'You must have a clear conscience.'

'I wish!' Mum laughed. 'Would you like some breakfast?'

'In a sec.' Sam sat down in an armchair. 'Planning on going somewhere?' he said, nodding at Mum's books.

'I thought you were probably fed up with hanging round here all day,' Mum said. 'There's an interesting country house not far away – Aldergrove Hall.'

'Interesting in what way?'

'In a country house sort of way – antiques, paintings, formal gardens.'

Sam pulled a face. Mum was a heritage addict, which accounted for her membership of the National Trust, but Sam wasn't so keen. Over the years he'd trailed around loads of houses that were basically the same, successions of rooms that felt empty despite being jam-packed with things. Heritage was cordoned off with silk ropes and do-not-touch labels.

'We don't have to go,' said Mum, 'not if you don't feel up to it.'

Sam had no desire whatsoever to visit Aldergrove

Hall, but he knew how disappointed his mother would be if he said no, and it might take her out of herself for a few hours.

'I'm OK,' he said. 'Let's go and see how the other half used to live.'

Mum beamed. 'What can I get you for breakfast?'

'Just coffee.'

'You need more than that, Sam. Your drugs work better if they're taken with food.'

'If my drugs work any better, I'll disappear entirely,' Sam said.

It was another fine day. They drove along narrow roads lined with tall hedges and overhanging trees. The leaves on the trees were bright and fresh. Gateways in the hedgerows gave glimpses of fields hazed with green, and flocks of sheep with new-born lambs frisking around. Sam recognized the irony – new life was beginning while his life was coming to an end – but didn't feel bitter.

Aldergrove Hall was clearly signposted at every junction, and there was no mistaking the main entrance – an impressively massive pair of iron gates supported by stone pillars. Each pillar was topped with a statue of a seated lion holding a shield in its front paws. The lions were pocked and weather-beaten, their eyes blinded by clumps of lichen.

Beyond the gates, a driveway swept up to a large house that looked as if it had started off small, but had gradually been added to over the years. The additions were in wildly differing styles – Georgian windows, a Gothic turret, a porch that resembled a miniature Greek temple, a Victorian extension in dove-grey and orange brick – leaving Sam with the impression that the house couldn't make up its mind which time it belonged in, but somehow it was naggingly familiar, and the familiarity grew stronger as he drew closer.

At the end of the driveway, Mum pulled up in an almost deserted car park, and they entered Aldergrove Hall. The ticket desk in the entrance doubled as a souvenir shop, so it was possible to buy souvenirs without actually touring the house, but Sam doubted if anybody bought anything. The erasers and bookmarks with *Aldergrove Hall* printed on them were deeply sad.

The main hallway was pretty much as Sam had expected.

Check your wood panelling and suit of armour, he thought. Check your large portraits of fat guys wearing clothes that are too tight. Check your stuffed animal heads.

There was a strong smell of furniture polish and air freshener, and an underlying fustiness. Sam had noticed how quickly even modern houses became dilapidated when they were unoccupied. His pet theory was that houses tapped the energy of the people who lived in them to maintain their fabric. When the energy was taken away, decay set in, and it was happening to Aldergrove Hall, in spite of all the National Trust's careful maintenance.

No focus, thought Sam. No point. This house is lonely.

Like the outside, the interior was a jumble of left-overs from different eras, as though a junk shop had been ransacked and its contents stuck into the house at random. Sam followed his mother through a book-lined study into a dining room, and then a drawing room. The drawing room was bright, light pouring in through French windows that led on to a set of steps going down into a sunken garden. The room was dominated by a grand piano that had been polished until it shone like a mirror, but Sam hardly noticed it because something grabbed his attention and wouldn't let go.

On one wall of the room hung a full-length portrait of Marion, wearing the white satin dress she'd worn the night he met her on the jetty. Her eyes looked quizzical, her lips were parted and Sam felt that she was about to step out of the frame and talk to him. The painting pulled him across the room. He stood in front of it and stared.

She's real, he thought. Or she *was* real. I haven't been hallucinating, I've been *meeting* someone.

Then he noticed the printed label below the portrait:

Marion Aldergrove-Freelong (1898–1919)
This portrait was completed shortly before the subject died of Spanish Influenza in the Great Epidemic of 1918–19.

Mum came up behind Sam, read the label and said, 'Oh, what a shame! She's so lovely.'

Something whirled in Sam's skull, and the room pitched like the deck of a boat riding a rough sea. He swayed.

'Sam?' said Mum. 'Is it too much for you? Do you want to go back to the cottage?'

Sam's voice sounded thick in his ears as he said, 'No. I'm tired after last night. I think I'll go outside and sit in the sun.'

'Shall I come with you?'

'You carry on. I'll be all right.'

Mum gave Sam a searching look.

'Really,' Sam insisted. 'I don't feel ill, just shattered.'

'But—'

'Mum,' Sam said sharply, 'cut me some slack, OK?'

The hurt in Mum's face made Sam feel guilty, but he badly needed to be on his own.

Sam had lied about not feeling ill. When he got outside, the heat waves radiating from the walls of the house and the ground made it seem as though the world were dissolving, and he felt that he was about to dissolve too. His illness had launched a surprise assault on him, and he had to find some quiet place where he could gather his strength for a counterattack.

You're not going to die yet, he told himself. Not yet and not here.

He followed a sign to the gardens and soon found himself in a shadowy avenue between two yew hedges. The shadows brought some welcome relief from the heat, but the air was still so heavy that it was like breathing thin soup. Sam passed through an archway that had been clipped in the hedge on his left, and entered a walled garden flagged with honey-coloured stones. Herbs grew in a circular raised bed, and he caught the savoury scent of sage mixed with the sweetness of lavender. Against one wall was a stone bench. Next to it, a wall-mounted basin was fed by a jet of water streaming from the mouth of a moulded-lead lion-mask. Sam walked around the herb bed, sat on the bench and looked into the basin. Light flashed hypnotically on the water. Below the surface, water boatmen hauled themselves along with their oar-shaped front legs.

The stillness of the light turned the garden into a painting. The jet of water from the lion's mouth was a frozen arc of silver, and the water boatmen in the basin were caught like flowers in perspex. The stillness only lasted for an instant before Marion stepped through the archway.

Ten

She was wearing a white cotton dress that glowed in the sunshine and her hair was loose. She hurried over to Sam, sat on the bench, placed her hands on his shoulders and kissed him. At the end of the kiss, she leaned back and looked closely at him. 'Your uniform is most becoming, Lieutenant Rawnsley,' she said.

Sam glanced down at himself and saw that he was dressed in a khaki jacket, beige jodhpurs and brown riding boots. 'No more games, Marion,' he said. 'It's too late.'

Marion smiled mischievously. 'But surely, too late is precisely the time when we need games most.'

Sam grunted. 'What I need just now is some answers,' he said. 'What's going on?'

'You are drawing closer to me,' said Marion. 'That is why the stillness is shorter than it was before.'

'And what will happen to me?'

'You will leave me and go to fight in France,' she said, a little stiffly.

Sam had a flash of intuition. 'I'll get killed there, won't I?'

Marion nodded. 'And then you'll return to me. We'll sit in this garden again, and we shall always be together.'

Her tone was measured and matter-of-fact, as if death were no more than a trip to the supermarket.

Sam stared at her in amazement. 'How can you be so calm, Marion? I've read the label under your portrait – you die too!'

'Only if you don't come back to me,' said Marion. 'You must trust me, Sam. Remember what I told you on the night of the ball? You have a rare gift. You can make anything happen.'

Sam laughed incredulously. 'Including miracles – like coming back from the dead?'

'One cannot escape from death,' said Marion, 'but one can escape from time. How long is a dream, Sam?'

This proved to be a surprisingly tricky question, and Sam fell silent as he thought about it. Eventually he said, 'I don't know – no one does. Time doesn't work the same way in dreams as it does when you're awake.'

Marion beamed at him. 'Exactly!' she said. 'Outside oneself a few hours pass, but within the dream one can live an entire lifetime, and more than one lifetime if the dream is deep enough. The choice is yours.'

'I have a *choice*?' Sam snorted.

'You can remain in time and reconcile yourself to the course your illness will take, or you can come outside time with me,' said Marion.

'How can I do that?'

'When you are ready, you will know.'

Sam shook his head. 'You make it sound easy.'

'It will not be easy, Sam,' Marion said, taking his hand in hers. 'You will have to leave all that you know and all those whom you love. But there will be other things to know, and ours is a love that will never fail, I promise you.'

Sam gazed at Marion's hand. He knew it as well

as his own, knew that the scar on her forefinger had been made by the metal hinge of a desk lid, knew the patterns of the lines on her palm. 'You're all of this, aren't you?' he said. 'You're the house, the river, the trees—'

'And so are you,' Marion interrupted. 'I would not be here if you were not here. I cannot live without you.'

'You mean that if I stop thinking about you, you won't exist?'

Marion clutched his hand so tightly that her knuckles showed white. 'Don't lose me, Sam!' she pleaded. 'We are our only chance of happiness. You are all I have, and I am all that you have.'

She went away, leaving Sam on his own with the scent of the herbs, and the trickling sound of water, and the sunlight on the stone of the bench.

Mum came into the garden, smiling apprehensively. 'I gave up on the house,' she said. 'I'd rather be with you.' She sat beside Sam and looked round at the herb bed. 'This is nice.'

'It's better than looking at furniture,' Sam said. 'I'm sorry I was ratty with you before. I know I don't often tell you, but I do love you, Mum. I want you to know in case something happens.'

Mum shuddered. 'Don't do that, Sam.'

'What?'

'It sounds as if you're saying goodbye.'

'Every day is goodbye,' said Sam.

'We'll sit in this garden again.'

Marion's words echoed through Sam's mind for the rest of the day and long after he went to bed. He could remember exactly how she'd said it, the certainty in her voice, the seriousness of her expression. She hadn't been teasing him, but speaking what she genuinely believed was the truth.

Outside an owl hooted, and there was the feeling of the river coursing through the night, but Sam was only vaguely aware of them. He thought of the seasonal cycle, spiral galaxies, the solar system spinning around the sun, like electrons circling a nucleus. According to his digital watch, time moved in a straight line, second following second in strict sequence. Some scientists theorized that linear time had come into existence at the moment of the Big Bang, and that it was a side-effect of the expanding universe. At some remote point in the future, the universe would have used up all the energy from the explosion that had formed it, and then the force of gravity would make it shrink.

Does that mean that time will go backwards? Sam asked himself. Will I live my life again the wrong way round? And once the universe reaches its starting point, will there be another Big Bang?

The universe might have repeated itself thousands of times. Perhaps there had been many Sams, Marions and walled gardens. In his head he heard Marion say, *'I find the wisest course of action is to simply accept things for what they are.'*

Sam had done a lot of accepting recently. He'd accepted the diagnosis of his illness and the nearness of death. He'd accepted medication, though it had appeared to cost him his sanity. Why shouldn't he accept Marion's promise?

Let go! Sam urged himself. Give your death to someone else and hitch a ride on the merry-go-round of time. If you never leave, how can you return?

Aloud, he said, 'I'm ready now.'

Eleven

Jill Rawnsley hadn't had a decent night's sleep for weeks, and the heavy thud from Sam's room brought her instantly awake. 'Sam?' she called. 'Are you all right?'

No answer.

Jill scrambled out of bed, went to Sam's door and rapped her knuckles against it. 'Sam?'

The silence turned ominous. Jill entered the room and switched on the light.

Sam lay on the floor, tangled in his duvet. Jill crossed the room, crouched beside him and pressed her fingers to his wrist to check his pulse; it was still beating.

'Sam?'

He was breathing heavily. His eyelids were slightly parted, showing the whites and not the irises of his eyes.

It was what Jill had been expecting and dreading. She wanted to scream and beat her head against something hard. Instead she forced herself to remain calm, went back to her bedroom, took a mobile phone from her handbag and called Emergency Services for an ambulance.

Twelve

David Rawnsley's nightmare began the moment that he took his ex-wife Jill's call from the hospital, and went on from there, stretching time out into for ever. He caught the next available train from Edinburgh and sat staring out of the window, seeing nothing. A robot version of him bought sandwiches and coffee from the trolley service, and ate and drank without tasting anything.

The train made so many stops that he lost count. Passengers got on and off. A man sitting opposite attempted to start a conversation, but gave up when his only response was an empty stare. David's mind was too blank to make any sense of what the man said.

He tried to block his memories, but they came anyway: holding the tiny squalling miracle that Sam had been, minutes after he was born; teaching Sam to ride a bicycle in the local park; the accusing look in Sam's eyes when the marriage had broken up; the awkward, faltering contact they'd had ever since. The thing inside him that loved Sam howled and shrieked, and tore itself with its fangs and claws, but the rest of him was still, and that made David afraid. The pain hadn't hit him yet, but when it did he knew that it would be massive and he wasn't sure that he'd be able to cope.

I don't want to do this, he thought. I want to run to where this isn't happening.

But there was no way out. None of his visions of the future had included his son dying before he died himself. David was in unknown territory, and there were no footpaths or signposts to show him the way through.

After the train arrived at its terminus, David took a taxi across the painted hardboard stage-set that was supposed to be London. The taxi stopped at a set of traffic lights. The driver looked into his rear-view mirror and said, 'Come far?'

'From Edinburgh,' said David.

The driver pursed his lips to show that he was impressed. 'You must've left early. Business trip?'

'No,' David said. 'My son's dying.'

The driver didn't talk after that.

At the apartment block, David didn't bother going to the flat. He went straight to the parking lot, collected his car and drove through heavy traffic to Chiswick, where he joined the M4. His eyeballs felt gritty and his mouth was dry, but at last he felt that he was doing something instead of being dependent on others. It took a massive effort to resist the temptation to speed, but if he was stopped by the police it would use up precious time.

David left the motorway at Reading, and promptly got lost in the tortuous one-way system. He had to go round again before he spotted the signs for the Royal Berkshire Hospital. When he finally arrived there he thought that he must have made a mistake, because the facade of the building looked more like a museum than a hospital – all fluted pillars and classical porticoes – but once inside he had no doubts as to where he was. Long concrete corridors led into even longer concrete corridors, all smelling of disinfectant, grief and fear.

When David reached the Intensive Care ward, a painfully hard lump came into his throat. A nurse showed him to the room.

He saw an imitation Sam lying in bed, propped up on pillows. It couldn't be the real Sam, because the real Sam didn't have blotchy skin, or tubes in his nostrils, mouth and arms. The real Sam wasn't wired to a monitor that measured his life in jagged lines.

There was someone else in the room, a ragged bird of a woman slumped on a chair beside the bed. David thought that she must be a cleaner, but then she stood up, spoke his name and he realized that she was Jill.

'I'm sorry it took me so long,' David said.

'It can't be helped,' said Jill, her voice sounding as if nothing could be helped.

'Has he regained consciousness?'

'No.'

'Is he going to?'

'No one can tell me. I don't think they know,' Jill said.

David wanted to hold her, to stop the progress of the desert of loneliness that was expanding inside him, but he didn't think that Jill would appreciate it, and if she pushed him away he might feel worse than he did already. He stepped over to the bed and touched Sam's face. There was no reaction.

'D'you remember—?' said David.

'I remember everything,' Jill said.

Sam's head stirred. His eyes darted from side to side beneath their closed lids.

'What's happening?' said David, alarmed.

'Rapid Eye Movement,' Jill said. 'The doctor says it shows that he's dreaming. It must be a good dream. He doesn't seem to want to wake from it.'

David didn't feel as if he was crying, but tears came out of his eyes. 'I'm sorry, Jill,' he said. 'There aren't words, are there?'

'No.'

'I wish—'

'I'm out of wishes,' Jill said. 'Prayers too.'

David heard his father telling him to pull himself together, and gave it his best shot. 'I know this is going to seem pretty callous, but d'you think . . . ?'

Jill bared her teeth. 'He's not a bloody pet, David, he's my son!' she hissed. 'It's his life. Let him find his own ending.'

David couldn't meet her eyes. He looked at the monitor and listened to its steady beep as he wept silently.

PART TWO

Thirteen

A sudden attack of giddiness swirled Sam to the brink of darkness. Instinctively he closed his eyes and clenched his fists. Convinced that he was in the act of dying, he clung on to the last thing he had left, his sense of himself.

The giddiness steadied. He felt solid ground under his feet and cold air on his face. The sound of voices made him open his eyes.

He was standing in a railway station. Beyond the far end of the platform, a clump of trees was a smudge on a skyline the colour of drizzle. He was surrounded by soldiers in khaki uniforms. Some stood in groups, others were seated on kit bags and almost all of them were smoking cigarettes. Most of the soldiers were boys and, by the look of it, new to smoking. They held their cigarettes awkwardly and puffed without inhaling. Though they chatted cheerfully and laughed loudly, their tension was unmistakable.

As Sam glanced from soldier to soldier, memories formed in his mind, like flakes of crystal coming out of a saturated solution, and he found that he could put a name to every face – Luxton, Ratcliff, Clemo, Dibble, Jones, Batt, Gray – he knew them all.

'My God, they're so young!' Sam murmured.

'They'll shape up soon enough, sir,' said a voice at his side.

Sam turned his head to look and saw a man with three stripes on the sleeve of his jacket. It was the same man who he'd seen in the dreams about the embankment and the summer field. There was no mistaking him, even though, beneath his cap, his hair had been brutally cropped to blue stubble.

Sam heard himself say, 'You think so, Sergeant Springer?' and hardly recognized the voice as his own.

The sergeant nodded curtly. 'They're bound to

have the wind-up at first, sir, but once they go into action, they'll give the Hun a bloody nose.'

'All over by Christmas, eh?'

The sergeant scowled. 'That's what the papers said this time last year, sir. You shouldn't believe everything they print in the papers.'

'Don't you read the papers, sergeant?'

'Only the casualty lists, sir.'

Sam felt as though he'd been put in his place. Sergeant Springer was an experienced professional soldier who'd served in the Boer War. In training camp he'd proved invaluable – a solid, dependable type with a remarkable talent for scrounging – but there was also something intimidating about him.

'Yes,' said Sam. 'The casualty lists make rather sombre reading, don't they?'

'You can't fight wars without men getting killed and wounded, sir. I found that out at Spion Kop.'

For a moment, Sergeant Springer's face was somewhere else.

'I've no doubt you did,' Sam said respectfully. 'What was it like out there in South Africa?'

'Bloody difficult to stay alive, sir,' said Sergeant Springer.

Captain Charvil walked along the platform, his progress marked by a ripple of salutes which he acknowledged by touching the peak of his cap with the tip of his swagger-stick. His uniform, tailored by a firm in Savile Row, was immaculate and his riding boots had been buffed up until they looked wet. When he reached Sam and the sergeant, they came to attention.

'Stand easy,' said Captain Charvil. 'The train will arrive at two pip-emma, so you'd better get the company fallen in. First-class carriages are for officers only and privates should give up their places to NCOs when requested to do so.'

'Aren't the officers going to travel with the men, sir?' said Sam.

Captain Charvil's laugh was hard and humourless. 'Certainly not!' he snorted. 'Overfamiliarity with the men breeds insubordination, Lieutenant Rawnsley. Carry on.'

'Sir!' said Sam, snapping off a salute.

Captain Charvil returned the salute and carried on down the platform.

'Odd, isn't it?' said Sam, thinking aloud. 'The men are good enough to order into battle, but not good enough to share a railway carriage with officers.'

'The captain's right, sir,' Sergeant Springer said. 'Treat 'em firmly and they'll walk over hot coals for you. Be kind to 'em, and you'll wind up in Queer Street.'

On the train, Sam jammed himself into a compartment with a group of other lieutenants. He knew some to speak to, others only by sight. They talked animatedly about the war, except for Subaltern Erskine, the second-lieutenant of D company. He slouched in a corner near the window, took glum sips from a silver hipflask and appeared to take no interest in anybody else.

The conversation came around to battlefield wounds. Several of the lieutenants displayed a morbid interest in the subject.

'I dread being wounded in the back,' said one. 'I wouldn't want anyone to think I'd got windy and run away.'

'I couldn't agree more, old man,' said another. 'One must keep one's face towards the enemy as much as possible. An arm or a leg wound is best, plenty of meat for the bullet to pass through. I met a chap who'd been shot in the arm. He told me that the doctors made an absolutely splendid job of patching him up. He was awarded the D.S.O. and transferred to some pen-pushing job in Whitehall, so he's safely out of it for the duration.'

'I should hate to lose an arm or a leg,' said a third, 'or even worse, both legs. I couldn't bear the shame of the burden it would place on my family. If I'm to be killed, let it be by a good clean head-shot, or let me be blown to pieces by a shell. That way, I'd know nothing about it. I heard of a fellow, a cavalry officer, who had his bottom jaw taken off by a piece of shrapnel. Unfortunately, the poor devil survived. If that happened to me, I'd beg the doctors for an overdose of morphine.'

Subaltern Erskine stirred and said, 'How could you, with no bottom jaw?'

'I'd write it out on a sheet of paper,' came the reply. 'What would you do in that situation, Erskine?'

'I don't know and I don't care,' Erskine said, struggling to his feet. 'What does it matter anyhow? We're already as good as dead. We've been dead since the moment we signed up, and anyone who doesn't understand that is a damned fool. Now if you'll excuse me, I'm going to take a turn along the corridor to stretch my legs.'

After Erskine had left the compartment, someone let out a low whistle and said, 'What an extraordinary thing! You don't think old Erskine has a touch of LMF, do you?'

LMF, thought Sam. Lack of moral fibre. Army code for cowardice.

But Erskine hadn't sounded cowardly, more as if he'd resigned himself to something that the other lieutenants hadn't considered. Intrigued, Sam left his seat and went out into the corridor.

Erskine was at the far end of the carriage. He'd lowered the window of the door and was gazing out at the bleak landscape as it rolled by. Sam went to stand next to him.

'Are you quite all right, Erskine?'

'I was listening to the wheels on the track,' said

Erskine. 'When I went on holiday by train as a child, I used to imagine that the wheels were saying we'll-soon-be-there, we'll-soon-be-there.'

As tactfully as he could manage, Sam said, 'I hope you won't take offence, Erskine, but you should be more careful about what you say. The other fellows are getting the wrong end of the stick about you.'

'And how d'you know there's a right end?' Erskine asked drily.

'Because I'm rather of your opinion myself. Did you mean it about our being dead since we joined up?'

'Yes,' said Erskine. 'I find the thought comforting. To volunteer as a soldier is to choose death over life. If one accepts that one is going to be killed, then there's nothing to be afraid of. It's as though the worst has already happened. We're separated from our homes, our loved ones and everything that made us what we are. All we can share is our otherness.'

This made sense to Sam. 'I was seriously ill a while ago,' he said. 'Everyone was certain that I was going to die, and no one was more certain than I. I was apart from everything, and people treated me as though I were apart. I didn't feel that I belonged anywhere. But now, facing all that we're about to face, I feel connected with things again.'

'At one with a world outside the world you once knew,' said Erskine.

'Exactly. What line of work were you in before the war?'

Erskine shrugged. 'That's in the past, and I've let the past go. There's nothing for me but the present moment. Yesterday is as far away as tomorrow.'

The rhythm of the train wheels altered as the points switched them onto another line.

A different track, thought Sam. I'm on a different track.

The train arrived at Southampton at nightfall, and several hours of frantic activity followed. After a roll call had been taken, the men marched to the docks to join the rest of their Division. Meals were provided by mobile field kitchens, and eaten in an empty warehouse that had been hurriedly converted into a mess hall. Then came the tedious process of embarking a thousand men in full kit onto two ships.

The ship carrying Sam's company cast off at ten o'clock. It had been fitted with searchlights, and once the ship had cleared the Solent, they were switched on. Sam stood on deck and watched the beams of light sweep across the sky and over the surface of the sea, searching for enemy aircraft and submarines.

Like blades, he thought. Like wings. Like the stare of gorgons.

The sea was calm, and in the searchlights' glare the same shade of green as Marion's eyes. Sam remembered the closeness of her kisses. It hadn't been the first time that he'd kissed a girl, but it had been the first time that a kiss had meant anything.

The wind shifted, carrying with it the distant rumble of an artillery barrage. Far off in the night, pale flickers lit the bases of low-lying clouds.

Sam shivered. There was no going back now.

Fourteen

The ships docked at Le Havre and the men disembarked. They formed ranks and set out on the two-mile march to the rail head, their boots clumping in perfect time on the cobbled roads. A fine rain fell, casting haloes around the gas lamps. Despite the weather and the lateness of the hour, townspeople turned out to cheer and wave. Some troops began to whistle *La Marseilleise* and others sang along, improvizing words.

'We're marching off to join the Fro–o–nt!

'We're marching off to—

'Join the Front!'

But the singing soon grew ragged as the day's long hours of travel began to tell. Soldiers fell asleep as they marched and stumbled out of step. Sergeants barked out sharp reprimands and issued threats of extra latrine duties. Somehow the Division managed to stay together, and they reached the rail head with few stragglers. The troops clambered aboard the waiting trains whose locomotives hissed and smoked like dragons.

Sam found himself a seat, set his cap over his face and fell asleep almost immediately.

In the dream, Sam was leaning on the mantelpiece of a fireplace in a drawing room. A log fire crackled in the hearth, and outside the French windows, a sunken garden was white with frost. The drawing-room door opened and Marion appeared, her eyes radiant. She ran across the room, flung her arms around him and squeezed him tightly.

'I thought you were in camp,' she said.

'I was,' said Sam, 'but I've been issued with a five-day pass.'

Marion stiffened and took a step back.

'Aren't passes issued to soldiers shortly before they're sent into action?' she said.

'Yes.'

'You're going to France!' Marion said dismally.

'I'm afraid I'm not allowed to reveal my destination.'

Anger glowed in Marion's eyes.

'Don't be ridiculous, Sam!' she snapped. 'Of course you're being sent to France – where else would you be sent? I suppose you've come to say goodbye.'

'I have.'

'Then say it and be gone.'

'There was another matter I wanted to discuss with you.'

Marion registered the graveness in Sam's voice and laughed mockingly.

'Why, Sam!' she said. 'One might almost imagine that you were about to propose to me.'

'No, it's not that,' said Sam. 'Quite the contrary, in fact. I want matters to be clear between us.'

'Everything is perfectly clear. You regard me as a friend, and nothing more.'

'You know that isn't true, Marion!' Sam protested. 'You know my feelings for you, as I know yours for me, but yours is a free spirit, and it is important to me that it remains free. This time next week I shall be – well, somewhere else. I don't know when, or if, I shall return. It may be that, in my absence, you may meet another whom you like better than me. Should that happen, you mustn't give me a thought.'

'Not give you a thought?' Marion exclaimed. 'What else shall I do but think of you, Sam? While you are gone it will be as though a part of me were missing.'

'The best of me will be with you,' Sam assured her. 'Only the soldier is going away.' He turned to the fire and poked one of the logs with the toe of his boot, releasing a galaxy of sparks.

The dream ended in the banging of carriage doors, and a French porter bawling out the name of a station.

The company was billeted in the stable of a farmhouse. The house had been hit by a shell and all but demolished. Officers' quarters were up in the hayloft; the men were to sleep on straw in the stalls on the ground floor. Lance-Corporal Clemo, the cook, rigged up a tarpaulin outside, set up his stove and brewed tea. The tea was mixed with sugar and milk and passed around in a bucket into which the men dipped their dixie cans.

Sam and Captain Charvil's tea was served by Private Cross, the captain's batman. He'd arrived at the billet two days previously, swept and scrubbed the loft, erected a pair of camp beds and strung a blanket to divide the space into two rooms. Empty cartridge-boxes provided tables, and Cross had managed to find two chairs. One was an old armchair with a dirty cloud of horsehair stuffing protruding from its back, the other was a chipped kitchen-chair. Captain Charvil lowered himself into the armchair with a loud sigh.

'I hope everything's satisfactory, sir,' said Cross. 'I've made it as comfortable as possible.'

'You've done well, Cross,' the captain replied. 'You may fall out now. Wake me at five-thirty sharp. Lieutenant Rawnsley and I will require morning coffee. Arrange it with Clemo.'

'Yes, sir. Sleep well, sir.'

After Cross had gone, the captain looked around and said, 'Home sweet home, eh? Hardly The Ritz, is it?'

'Quite luxurious compared with the men's quarters,' Sam observed.

'The men will manage. After their first night in the trenches, they'll dream of their stable stalls. You should select one of the privates to act as your batman, Rawnsley. I'm surprised that you haven't already.'

'I'm not sure that I need a batman, sir,' said Sam. 'I can rub along pretty well on my own.'

Captain Charvil looked puzzled. 'But every officer must have a batman,' he insisted. 'The men expect it. You have servants at home, don't you?'

Sam nodded. 'Yes, but that's rather different.'

'Different? In what way?'

'I don't expect my servants to fight, sir.'

Captain Charvil produced a bottle of whiskey from his kit and began to peel the lead foil from around the cork. 'I say, Rawnsley, you're not one of those socialist types, are you?'

'No, sir. It just doesn't seem fair to ask a man to be a servant as well as a soldier.'

'All's fair in love and war, don't you know,' sniggered the captain. 'And the men don't mind. They see it as a perk. After all, if a chap's polishing one's boots and so on, he doesn't have to be out on parade with the others. I generally slip Cross half a crown a week, and he's glad to get it.'

'Even so, sir . . .'

Captain Charvil uncorked the whiskey, sloshed some into his tea and offered the bottle to Sam. 'Take a drop, Rawnsley. What's the old joke? The whiskey takes away the taste of the tea, and the tea takes away the taste of the whiskey.'

'I'd rather not, just now, if you don't mind, sir,' said Sam.

'Suit yourself. But you *will* choose a batman, Lieutenant. First thing in the morning – and that's an order.'

'Yes, sir.'

The captain gulped down his tea and glanced at his watch. 'Hardly worth getting my head down, but I suppose I should,' he said with a yawn. 'I advise you to do the same.'

'I managed to get some sleep on the train, sir. Would it be all right if I stayed up a while longer to write?'

'A letter, you mean?'

'No, I'm keeping a sort of diary.'

'Then be careful about what you put in it,' the captain warned. 'If it should fall into enemy hands—'

'I shall be careful, sir,' Sam said.

He found the notebook that Marion had given to him as a goodbye present, the same blue, black and white covered book that he'd dreamed of in another life. He took a pencil from the breast pocket of his tunic and wrote.

It's getting stronger, like I'm starting to feel that Lieutenant Rawnsley is really me and the other Sam, the one who got sick, is the illusion. I don't know how I picked up on all this detail, probably from books and—

The point of the pencil hesitated. Sam had been going to write about movies and TV documentaries that he'd watched, but as soon as he thought of the words *movies* and *TV*, they lost their meaning.

The fantasy had changed gear and was carrying him further and further away from the person he'd once been.

Fifteen

Dawn was breaking grey when the soldiers turned out on inspection parade the next morning. Sam accompanied Captain Charvil on his rounds, passing his comments on to Sergeant Springer who jotted them down in a notebook. At training camp, Captain Charvil had been a stickler when it came to inspections, and he now demonstrated that there was to be no relaxation of his exacting standards. If a soldier's rifle or kit was dirty, the captain sentenced him to extra duties.

After the parade, the men fell out to have their breakfast.

'I daresay you consider me to be something of a martinet, Rawnsley,' the captain said. 'But we can't afford to let our standards slip. An untidy soldier is a sloppy soldier, and a sloppy soldier is a menace to himself and all those who depend on him.'

'I'm sure you're right, sir,' said Sam.

Captain Charvil smiled grimly. 'I'm not an unreasonable man, however. I believe in being equally unfair to every man under my command.' The captain turned his head and called out, 'Sergeant Springer!'

The sergeant left his tin plate of bread and bacon and marched over.

'Sir?'

'Lieutenant Rawnsley here requires a batman. Whom would you recommend?'

The sergeant thought for a moment, then said, 'Private Houndsome, sir. He's an honest lad, very biddable.'

'Have him report to the lieutenant after breakfast.'

'Yes, sir!'

Sam rankled at this, but didn't dare to contradict Captain Charvil in front of the men.

*   *   *

Houndsome was a tall, slim young man with brown eyes, black hair and a smooth complexion that strongly suggested he hadn't started shaving yet. He seemed pleased to have been chosen as a batman, but was extremely nervous. Sam noticed that Houndsome's hands were shaking, and tried to put him at his ease.

'Whereabouts are you from, Houndsome?' he enquired.

'Wokingham, sir,' said Houndsome. 'That's in Berkshire, that is.'

'Oh, I know it. My family lives not far from there. How are you finding life in the army?'

'Suits me fine, sir,' said Houndsome. 'I've put on six pounds since I joined. We don't eat that regular at home, y'see, sir.'

'And what made you volunteer?'

Houndsome seemed taken aback by the question. 'Well, sir,' he said, 'my old dad said he reckoned as how I ought to, and the local vicar said it was the duty of every able-bodied man to do his bit, and then a lot of my pals joined up, so it sort of seemed the right thing to do. My ma wasn't too keen though.'

'I can imagine,' said Sam. 'No more was mine. How old are you, Houndsome?'

Houndsome's eyes flicked from side to side and he licked his lips before he said, 'Seventeen, sir.'

'Seventeen?' Sam said dubiously.

Houndsome's shoulders sagged. 'To tell you the truth, sir, I won't be seventeen till next August, but what's a few months when there's a war on? It's being willing that matters, not how old you are, and I wanted a chance to make something of myself.'

Like a corpse? thought Sam. He said, 'You know that sixteen is below the legal age for enlistment?'

Houndsome nodded.

'By rights, you ought to be shipped back to Blighty,' Sam went on. 'But I shan't tell if you don't. We need all the men we can get. Thank you for being frank with me.'

'That's my ma, that is, sir,' said Houndsome. 'She brung me up to always tell the truth. "Tell the truth and shame the devil," she says.'

For the rest of the day, officers and men worked hard carrying out field exercises in open country. The land was mostly flat, but in the distance was a long ridge, high ground that was held by the Germans. There had been a British assault – a push – on the ridge the previous winter and the ridge had been taken with heavy casualties on both sides, but a German counterattack had thrown the British back where they had started.

During the field exercises, the men practised digging and repairing trenches, crossing obstacles while carrying heavy equipment and target-shooting. When rapid fire was ordered, a skilled rifleman was able to fire fifteen rounds a minute, but the German trenches were defended by machine guns whose rate of fire was far more rapid. The best the company could muster in reply was an old Maxim gun that was a leftover from Victorian times.

Sam wondered how on earth the British expected to succeed with such shoddy equipment, and the constant muddle. Most of the officers appeared blasé and assumed that the men would manage. This was brought home to Sam on the second evening at the billet. He followed Captain Charvil as he circulated among the men while their dinner was being served, and asked if they had any complaints. It was an invitation for the soldiers to comment on the quality of the food, which was generally dire, but Private Ratcliff had another matter on his mind.

'I wondered when we'd be getting steel helmets, sir,' he said.

'Steel helmets?' the captain exclaimed.

'Yes, sir. The Jerries have got 'em, so it stands to reason that we ought to have 'em as well, doesn't it, sir?'

Captain Charvil drew himself up to his full height, thrust his swagger-stick under his arm and bristled. 'Now look here, Ratcliff, I'll have no talk of that kind in my company, d'you understand? It's grit that will get us through this war, not steel helmets. They're heavy and they impair freedom of movement in the Front Line. They also give a soldier a false sense of security. The German Imperial Army's use of the steel helmet is a sign of its decadence and a symptom of Teutonic cowardice. Going into battle wearing steel helmets simply isn't fair play.'

'Yes, sir,' Ratcliff said subserviently. 'Sorry I spoke, sir.'

Fair play? thought Sam. Charvil makes it sound as if he's fielding a cricket team!

But Charvil's attitude provided Sam with an important insight. Most of the officers he'd met treated the war as sport, a game that had to be played according to the rules, no matter how much suffering and bloodshed it caused.

After dinner, the mail from home was distributed. Sam was given a letter and instantly recognized Marion's handwriting on the front of the envelope. He took the letter up into the hay loft, lit a lamp and opened the envelope with the point of his bayonet.

My dear Sam, the letter began. *How odd you must feel, and how alien everything must seem in a world so different from the one that you knew.*

Sam broke off to think for a minute. Marion was wrong. It was the other world that seemed alien to him now, as strange and distant as one of H.G. Wells' visionary stories of the future, filled with incomprehensible electrical machines and bizarre moral values.

He grunted and returned to the letter.

I miss you terribly and cannot keep thoughts of you

out of my mind. How I long to be with you in the herb garden again, to kiss you and hold your hand, and tell you that all is well. I promise you that once the nightmare is done, there will be many peaceful dreams. Each of us has his own reality, quite separate from anyone else's, and is condemned to live it through until the end. But you and I and can share realities, and it gives us a closeness that goes beyond the body and the spirit.

I am waiting for you, Sam. I ache to be near you.
Your loving Marion.

Captain Charvil climbed up the ladder from the ground floor. He glanced at Sam without appearing to see him, went over to the wooden crate that acted as a cupboard, took out his bottle of whiskey and poured a generous measure into a tumbler.

'What is it, sir?' Sam said.

Captain Charvil drank the whiskey in two gulps and wiped his mouth with the back of his hand. 'I've just had a message from a friend of mine at HQ. The word is that there's going to be a big push before too long, and we're likely to be a part of it.'

'Their big push or ours, sir?' asked Sam.

'Ours, if the rumours flying around can be

credited.' The captain poured himself another drink. 'Let's pray the Hun hasn't heard the rumours, or there'll be hell to pay,' he said.

Sixteen

The morning before Sam's company transferred up to the Front Line was spent in preparation. The men busied themselves in various ways: cleaning their weapons, drawing extra ammunition from the stores, writing letters home; a few even sought out the padre. Sam found it difficult to judge the soldiers' underlying mood until he spoke to Houndsome, who came up into the hayloft to pack away his gear.

'Anxious about going up the line, Houndsome?' Sam asked.

Houndsome smiled his slow, uncertain smile. 'Can't say as I've given it that much thought, sir, but I'm not what you'd call anxious, more wanting to get on with it. We've spent months parading, drilling and marching. Now all that's done with, and it's time for us to fight.'

'Do you hate the Germans?'

'No, sir,' said Houndsome. 'I reckon most of 'em are just ordinary working lads like me.'

'Then won't you mind having to kill them?'

'Don't know, sir. Haven't killed any yet.'

Which neatly summed up the quandary that Sam was facing. He'd never even been in a fist fight with anyone – could he really bring himself to draw his revolver and shoot a total stranger? During target practice he'd fired the pistol – a great lump of a thing with a recoil that made his wrist and shoulder ache afterwards. Sergeant Springer had given him some advice on how to use it – 'Aim at the feet, you'll hit your target in the belly. Aim for the belly, you'll hit him in the chest. Aim for the chest, you'll hit him in the head,' – but Sam wasn't sure that he'd be able to apply it. At three o'clock a corporal from another company reported to Captain Charvil, to act as a guide. He led the way through a maze of interconnected trenches. Here and there pieces of wood had been fixed to the walls, painted with names like 'Paradise Alley' and 'Lovers Lane'. The trenches were waterlogged, and in places the planks that had been laid down to provide firm footing were covered by mud to a depth of several inches.

After an hour's slow progress, the corporal called a halt and the company waited for darkness to fall. That wait was the most difficult ordeal so far for Sam. He could do nothing but crouch in a trench, knowing that he was well within range of German artillery, and uncomfortably aware that if he stood up and showed his head above the parapet, a German sniper would, as likely as not, blow out his brains.

What seemed like a lifetime of discomfort later, the guide declared, 'Time to move on. Remember, once we're in the communications trench, stay close together, keep well down and keep quiet. Jerry's rigged up a grenade catapult, and if he hears any interesting noises coming from our way, he's liable to drop a grenade right in your lap. Put out your fags and look lively.'

The going was treacherous. The planks of the walkway were invisible in the dark and those who took a wrong step found themselves up to their knees in mud. The trench twisted and bent back on itself, so that following it was like passing through the digestive tract of a huge animal. Up ahead, an orange star floated up into the night and burst into a blindingly white globe of light that wavered lazily as it fell.

The company froze and ducked into the shadows for cover, but the corporal hurried them on. 'Don't stop!' he urged. 'The trench is straight in front of you. At the double now!'

Sam made his way to the corporal's side. 'What's that light?' he demanded.

'A Very light, sir,' the corporal replied. 'Jerry fires 'em all night long at five-minute intervals so he can keep his eye on no man's land.'

More lights appeared along the whole length of the line, shrinking into the distance until they were too tiny to make out.

The men in the company that was standing down looked like grimy ghosts, hollow-eyed from lack of sleep, faces streaked with camouflage paint and mud, and they gave off vinegary waves of unwashed-body smell. Their commander, Captain Phelps, greeted Captain Charvil and Sam outside what he jokingly referred to as 'the office', a cramped room dug into the wall of a trench, furnished with a single camp bed and an empty wine bottle with a stub of candle jammed into its neck.

Once the formalities of the changeover had been completed, Captain Phelps became chatty. 'I say, Charvil old chap, you wouldn't happen to know if that push we've been hearing about is in the offing any time soon, would you?' he asked.

'Yes,' said Captain Charvil. 'As a matter of fact it's set for the eleventh.'

'Thought as much,' Phelps said. 'The Hun's been pretty sharp along this sector of the line just recently.'

'Sharp?'

Phelps nodded. 'They've brought some crack snipers into the line just opposite, and they take pot shots at anything they see. They've been a damned nuisance ever since we arrived. They shot two periscopes to smithereens, so some of my men had to make do with bits of mirror wired to the tips of their bayonets.'

'The corporal who brought us up from camp mentioned something about a grenade catapult,' said Sam.

Phelps rolled his eyes. 'Oh, Lord! That bloody thing has made our lives a misery. The Hun knows that the men try to get some rest between noon and four, so he lobs a couple of grenades over at about two o'clock to wake everybody up.'

'Any casualties?' said Captain Charvil.

'No, but you might not be so lucky,' Phelps said with grim humour. 'Whoever fires the catapult has just about got his eye in.'

'You think that the Germans might have got wind of the push?'

Phelps yawned loudly. 'I don't see why not, old chap, they seem to have got wind of everything else. The Hun isn't the worst problem though.'

'Then what is?'

'Rats!' Phelps exclaimed. 'I should say that every rat in Northern France is billeted hereabouts, and you should see the size of them. Bigger than cats. That's because of the extra food we've provided for them.'

'You mean that the men feed the rats?' Sam said, puzzled.

'Not in the way that you mean, old chap. The rats have been feeding on the corpses that were lost in no man's land after the battle last year. Some of the men think they've got the taste for human flesh, and it's been the devil of a job to stop them from shooting rats on sight. If they did, the Germans would think that we'd opened fire on them, they would fire back and there would be all kinds of unpleasantness. Can't have that sort of thing happening in a war, can we? Toodle-oo!'

Phelps and his company left the trenches, and Sam's company settled in. Officers were allowed to rest in four-hour shifts, but there was no rest for the men. They had to stay awake all night, taking turns with periscopes to keep a close watch on the Germans. Blankets were forbidden in the trenches for fear that if the troops were made too comfortable they would fall asleep and become vulnerable to attack.

The lack of blankets was a major hardship, for the night was bitterly cold as Sam discovered when he took the first watch. He patrolled the line, passing men who huddled together for warmth, blowing into their cupped hands. At one point, he met Sergeant Springer coming from the opposite direction.

'How are you holding up, sir?' said the sergeant.

'Pretty well,' Sam said. 'What are the Germans up to?'

'No good, sir, but they're not doing it anywhere that we can see.' Sergeant Springer tapped the shoulder of the man standing nearest to him. 'Dibble, lend Lieutenant Rawnsley your periscope for a moment.'

Sam took the periscope, gingerly raised it above the rim of the parapet and looked into the object mirror.

Lit by the stark glare of the Very lights, no man's land was as barren and bleak as the surface of the moon, and was coloured with various shades of grey, brown and black. There were shell holes everywhere, and shell holes within shell holes, some filled with rainwater. Strands of broken barbed wire were twisted into the air, and the only trees left standing were shattered stumps whose bark and branches had been blasted away by high explosive. Except for the faint fizzing of the burning flares, it was deadly silent.

Sam handed the periscope back to Private Dibble and turned to Sergeant Springer.

'Must have been a fine piece of farmland out there once, Sergeant,' said Sam.

The sergeant smiled, his teeth a pale gleam in the dark. 'And it will be again, sir,' he said. 'The Hun's machine guns will be bringing in the harvest before too long.'

Seventeen

With the dawn came a thick grey mist that formed a frost in no man's land, making it glitter in a way that was both attractive and sinister. At half-past five Sam, who was on his second watch, ordered Privates Batt and Foxton to bring up tea from the field kitchen in one of the communication trenches. The tea, when it came, wasn't particularly good, but the men were grateful for its warmth and clutched their dixie cans in both hands, letting the steam waft over their faces.

They're glad that they survived the night, Sam reflected, and it struck him that this was how men endured their time at the Front, by taking it one day at a time and celebrating each new morning.

At six o'clock Captain Charvil came on duty, and Sam accompanied him and Sergeant Springer as they carried out an inspection. As well as checking the men's weapons, this involved a foot-inspection, a precaution against the condition known as 'trench foot'. Captain Charvil discharged this duty with his customary rigour, and when he noticed the pulpy red swelling on the heel of Private Davies' left foot, his face whitened in anger.

'What's this, Davies?' the captain demanded.

'It's a chilblain, sir,' Davies replied.

'What d'you mean by it, Private?'

'I don't mean anything by it, sir,' said Davies. 'I always get chilblains on my feet in the cold weather, sir.'

Captain Charvil scowled. 'Are you a malingerer, Davies?'

'No, sir!'

'Did you cultivate this chilblain in the hope that I would send you back down the Line?'

'No, sir! I wouldn't do that, because the little beggar hurts, sir.'

Captain Charvil turned his head to Sam and said,

'Lieutenant Rawnsley, kindly instruct Sergeant Springer to place this man on latrine duty until further notice.'

'Yes, sir,' said Sam. 'Did you catch that, Sergeant?'

'Duly noted, sir,' the sergeant said.

After the inspection, breakfast was served. Houndsome brought Sam's to the dugout.

'What's on the menu this morning, Houndsome?' Sam asked.

'Porridge and sausages, sir,' said Houndsome.

'How is the porridge?'

'I'd tackle it with a bayonet rather than a spoon, sir.'

Sam laughed. 'And the sausages?'

'Opinions are divided over the sausages, sir. Some reckon as they've been made from cats, some say horses.'

'Didn't Clemo tell you?'

Houndsome pulled a face. 'I didn't ask, sir. I find it pays not to know.'

'Thank you for the advice, Houndsome. Off you go and have your own breakfast.'

'Very good, sir.'

When Houndsome had gone, Sam noticed a tension in the air. Captain Charvil was doggedly chewing his way through his porridge without the least sign of enjoyment and his eyes were staring sourly into the middle distance.

'You seem rather preoccupied, sir. Is everything all right?' Sam said.

'I'm thinking about Davies,' said Captain Charvil. 'I'm concerned about the effect he may have on the other men. It only takes one bad apple to spoil a whole barrel.'

'I'm not so sure that he is a bad apple, sir. I don't think that one *can* deliberately give oneself a chilblain.'

'You'd be amazed what men are capable of,' the captain said. 'I've heard of some cowardly types who shoot themselves in the foot to avoid combat.'

'Davies doesn't strike me as that sort, sir. He always pulled his weight in training camp.'

Captain Charvil gave Sam a cold glance. 'Training camp is one thing, Lieutenant, and the Front Line is quite another. Who knows how a man might act when he really finds himself up against it?'

'Have you had any experience of combat, sir?' Sam asked

A guilty expression crossed the captain's face, and he stroked his moustache with the tips of his fingers. 'Only on the rugger field,' he said. 'But I expect the principle will be much the same.'

Sam was about to congratulate the captain on his witty remark, when he realized that Charvil hadn't intended it as a joke.

'I'm sure you're right, sir,' Sam said.

Just before noon, Major Hutchins visited the trench and talked to Captain Charvil and Sam outside the dugout. Major Hutchins was tall and lanky, with a sharp nose and a muddy complexion. His cloudy blue eyes seemed to look straight through anyone he talked to.

'Settled in all right, Charvil?' said the major.

'Yes, sir.'

'Any problems?'

'None worth mentioning, sir.'

'Glad to hear it,' said the major. 'Now as you've probably surmised, I'm not simply paying a social call.

I have splendid news for you, Charvil. The general wishes to know the exact disposition of the enemy regiments we're facing, so he's decided to send a number of raiding parties across no man's land, the objective being to secure prisoners for interrogation. You'll be pleased to learn that your company has been chosen to take part in the operation. Five men should be enough – including an officer, of course. The raid will take place tonight at ten pip-emma. A green flare will be fired at nine forty-five to signal the commencement of a diversionary mortar attack to wrongfoot the enemy.'

Captain Charvil nodded. 'Yes, sir. I'll lead the men myself.'

'I rather think that wouldn't be appropriate, Charvil,' said the major. 'I'm sure that Lieutenant Rawnsley here will prove equal to the task.'

'Thank you, sir,' said Sam, though he didn't know why he was thanking the major. He'd been chosen to lead the raid because lieutenants were more expendable than captains.

'I wonder if you'd mind leaving the lieutenant and myself alone for a while, Charvil,' the major said smoothly. 'There are a few procedural matters I should like to discuss with him, and I'm sure you have duties that you're anxious to be about.'

Captain Charvil was clearly irritated at being excluded, but he came to attention and saluted before turning away.

When he was sure that the captain was out of earshot, Major Hutchins took a cigarette case from the breast pocket of his tunic, opened it and held it out to Sam.

'Care for one, Rawnsley?' he enquired.

'That's very decent of you, sir,' said Sam, sensing that more than a cigarette was on offer. The major had something unpleasant to say, and was hoping that an atmosphere of informality would soften the blow. He and Sam smoked in companionable silence for a few moments, then the major brushed a fragment of tobacco from his lower lip and said, 'Strictly *entre nous*, Rawnsley, there's more to tonight's raid than I let on. I judged it prudent not to say too much in Captain Charvil's presence, because the fewer people who know about it the better. We've received an intelligence report that the Germans may have brought gas-generating equipment into their line. You've heard about gas, I suppose?'

'Yes, sir,' said Sam. 'We're developing it ourselves, aren't we?'

'More's the pity!' the major said bitterly. 'Damned filthy stuff, gas, and not British somehow, but there we are. Anyhow, the point is, if the Germans have been supplied with gas, it could have serious implications for the push. So tonight, when you reach the enemy trenches, a search for gas equipment is to be your priority. Should you manage to take a prisoner, all well and good, but don't make it your primary concern. After the raid, you will report your findings directly to me, and under no circumstances are you to discuss them with anyone else. If word leaks out that the Germans have gas, it could sap the men's morale.'

'Understood, sir,' said Sam. 'But even if the Germans are capable of launching a gas attack, they're hardly likely to, are they? Gas is an offensive rather than a defensive weapon, isn't it?'

The major gestured with his cigarette, sending spirals of smoke twirling through the air. 'Offensive, defensive, who's to say? I only know that the general requires information and you're among the persons whom I'm deputing to obtain it.'

'Has the general been fully apprised of the use of gas on the battlefield, sir?' Sam said.

'Oh, I dare say he has,' said the major. 'The general's very thorough. He learned his trade with Kitchener at Omdurman. They're as thick as thieves, apparently.'

'But—'

The major leaned closer and spoke in a low voice. 'Look here, Rawnsley, you know this raid is unnecessary and so do I, but the general has a bee in his bonnet about gas, and it's our job to keep him happy. Is that understood?'

'Perfectly, sir.'

The major leaned back. 'Stout fellow! If I were you, I shouldn't be too conscientious tonight. Get over there, have a quick look around and then get back. No heroics.'

Sam was angry, not just because he'd been ordered to risk his life pointlessly, but because he'd have to put the lives of some of his men at risk. 'Might I ask you something, sir?' he said.

'Certainly.'

'In your estimation, what are our chances of success on the eleventh?'

The major sighed, and ground the stub of his cigarette against the dugout wall. 'Let me answer your question this way,' he said. 'The war has gone on for far longer than any of us expected, and the British public is becoming concerned about the number of casualties we've suffered. If we win a victory here, any sort of a victory, it will encourage the recruitment figures. Should we fail, the government may have to give serious consideration to the introduction of conscription, and that wouldn't be at all popular. The general can bring us the victory we need, if any man can.'

It was only an hour later, after Sam had given these words some thought, that it registered that the major hadn't answered his question. He'd given Sam the reasons behind the coming push, but had neatly avoided expressing his opinion of it.

In this war, Sam said to himself, it isn't what people say that matters, it's what they *don't* say.

Eighteen

Though Major Hutchins had deprived him of the chance to lead the raiding party, Captain Charvil soon showed that he was determined not to have all his thunder stolen by his junior officer, for when the midday meal – a thick stew containing chunks of gristly meat – was served, the captain sought Sam out.

'It's all arranged, Rawnsley,' he said.

'What is, sir?'

'The details of the raid. I've arranged them with Sergeant Springer. Here, look.' The captain took a clipboard from under his arm. Attached to it was a neatly sketched map of the area directly opposite the trench. 'You'll take Hocking, Gray, Jones and Sergeant Springer with you. Hocking and Gray will guard your flanks and provide you with any covering fire that proves necessary. Jones and Sergeant Springer will cut a way through the barbed wire, and then you and Sergeant Springer will enter the German trench. No one is to discharge his weapon unless you give the signal, which will be three sharp blows of your whistle. When the raid is completed, report directly to me.'

'I'm sorry, sir,' Sam said. 'I'm under orders from Major Hutchins to make my report to him.'

Captain Charvil turned as stiff and spiky as a hedgehog rolled into a ball. 'I see,' he said. 'The major's orders must take precedence over mine, I suppose.'

The captain's pride had evidently been hurt and Sam tried to put things right between them before they deteriorated any further. 'I'm most awfully sorry about this, sir,' he said. 'I know that you were keen to take command of the raid, but I think that Major Hutchins was correct in keeping you here.'

'Do you now?' the captain said sarcastically. 'Well as long as the major's orders meet with your approval, that's all right, isn't it, Lieutenant?'

Sam tried again. 'I think you may have

mis-understood me, sir,' he said. 'All I mean is that when the push begins, a lieutenant or so fewer will be neither here nor there, but the loss of a captain could be crucial. The company need you to lead them into battle.'

Captain Charvil pursed his lips and his shoulders lost some of their tension. 'I see what you mean, Rawnsley. That puts matters in quite a different light.'

'And forgive my raising this, sir, but by the same token wouldn't it be better to choose someone other than Sergeant Springer? Should anything happen to him, he'd be sorely missed.'

Captain Charvil smiled smugly. 'D'you speak German, Rawnsley?'

'No, sir, I'm afraid that I don't.'

'I thought not – but Sergeant Springer does. That will give you an advantage when it comes to taking prisoners.'

Sam thought, If in doubt, brown-nose! and said, 'I didn't realize that Sergeant Springer knew German, sir. You're quite right, it will give me an advantage.'

'Get to know the strengths and weaknesses of your men, Lieutenant,' the captain announced pompously.

'That's the first rule of how to think like a soldier.'

'I'll bear that in mind, sir,' Sam said.

Sam couldn't sleep during the rest period, so he passed the time by writing to Marion. It wasn't a letter – letters were subject to censorship and the censors would never let through what he wanted to say. He wrote in his notebook, knowing that if he didn't return from the raid, his possessions would be sent back to England and there was a chance that Marion might read his words.

Dear Marion,

You wouldn't believe the way this war is being run. The officers treat the men like dirt, and as far as they're concerned the privates in the line are just cannon fodder. There's a lot of talk about big pushes, rolling back the enemy and consolidating our position, but it's all rubbish. The war's being fought for the benefit of politicians, and they've given command to generals who haven't got a clue about modern warfare. The men deserve better.

Tonight I'm going to lead a raiding party into the

German line. My uniform is looking strange because I've had to take off all my badges and insignia, so the Germans won't know what regiment I'm in if I'm captured.

I think about you constantly and I want more time with you, other lives when we can be together, something other than this. War is senseless, boring, dirty and wasteful. It's the waste that sickens me the most, the waste of time and lives. And what does war ever achieve, apart from preparing the ground for another war? Isn't it ironic that this part of the world, that thinks it's so civilized, is involved in the killing of more people than at any other time in history? Or is that how we measure civilization, by the number we can kill long-distance?

But don't worry. I'm not going to let you down. I'll do as I'm told and be a good little soldier.

Love, Sam

P.S. I remember your kisses. Any chance of another, somewhere, somewhen?

At nine-thirty, Sam and the rest of the raiding party were in position, standing below the firing step. They were issued with a ration of rum, which was the customary practice for men going into action as rum was supposed to steady their nerves.

Or maybe get them drunk enough to make obeying a pointless order seem like a good idea, Sam thought. He drank his measure off in one gulp to avoid tasting it, but he couldn't avoid the long burn of the liquor passing down his throat and into his stomach.

The men's anxiety showed in different ways. Hocking and Gray whispered jokes to each other and giggled; Jones kept slightly apart and was silent, his eyes as wide and stunned as a fawn's. The only one who appeared calm was Sergeant Springer, and Sam engaged him in conversation to take his mind off his own fear, which was like an iron band being tightened across his chest.

'The captain tells me that you speak fluent German, Sergeant,' Sam said.

'I don't know about fluent, sir, but I know enough to get by.'

'Where did you pick it up?'

'The wife's family is German, sir. I've spent quite

a bit of time in Germany over the years. I've two nephews serving in the Kaiser's army.'

'That must be difficult for you.'

Sergeant Springer frowned. 'Difficult, sir?'

'You must feel that your loyalties are divided.'

'I'm not sure I follow you, sir.'

Sergeant Springer seemed reluctant to discuss his private life, but Sam's curiosity made him go on probing.

'What if, by some peculiar twist of fate, you were to meet one of your nephews tonight in the German trenches, charging at you with a fixed bayonet?'

Without hesitation, the sergeant said, 'I'd shoot him, sir.'

'To wound, or to kill?'

'That would depend on how much time I had, sir.'

'And would you have any compunction?'

The sergeant cocked his head to one side, like a sparrow eyeing a crumb. 'Beg pardon, sir?'

'Would you feel guilty?' Sam said.

'Guilt's a luxury you can't afford in battle, sir,' said the sergeant. 'It has to wait until the fighting's done.' His eyes left Sam's face and looked into the sky. 'Here we go,' he said.

Sam followed Sergeant Springer's gaze.

Away to their left, a green signal flare arced up into the night. When it reached its zenith, Sam heard the seal-bark sound of mortar fire, followed by flashes in the German trenches, the flat thump of exploding charges and the pattering of machine guns.

Sam made to get onto the firing step, but the sergeant held him back.

'It's not ten o'clock yet, sir. Give the Hun time to send reinforcements down the line, then we'll only have their skeleton guard to deal with.'

The sound of firing intensified and Sergeant Springer grinned. 'Seems like they've taken the bait, sir.'

Sam felt detached from himself. His fear was still there, but he refused to accept it – there was too much to do and too many people were depending on him.

Easy, Sam, you can do this, he thought. He looked at his wristwatch and saw, by the last light of a German flare, the second hand sweep up to the hour.

'Now!' he said.

He heaved himself up onto the firing step, then rolled over the sandbags into no man's land. With Sergeant Springer on his right and Private Jones on his left, he advanced at a crouching run towards a low wall, all that remained of a farm building. They reached it and ducked down, just as another German flare burst into light over their heads.

Sam looked over his shoulder and saw Hocking and Gray lying flat, almost indistinguishable from the churned mud around them. Beyond the wall stood the lines of barbed wire that reminded Sam of the briar thicket surrounding a sleeping princess in a fairy tale.

The flare fell to earth and sputtered out. In the darkness that followed, Sergeant Springer and Private Jones crawled forward and began to snip away with their wire cutters. Sam was right behind them, his pistol ready to return fire if they were spotted. Even with the noise of fighting in the background, it seemed impossible that no one in the German trench could miss the clicking of the cutters. In his imagination, Sam saw his head caught in the crosshairs of a sniper's telescopic sight and he expected a bullet to hit him at any second.

A hand clapped against his shoulder, making him start. Private Jones and Sergeant Springer were holding up the cut wire, making a tunnel for Sam to go through. He quickly holstered his revolver and scrabbled on his stomach, pushing himself along with his feet and elbows. When he was clear of the wire he waited for Sergeant Springer, then both men ran towards the German line, keeping low. They breasted the parapet and dropped down.

Sam's first impression of the German trench was how superior it was to its British equivalent. It was wider, more securely shored and the duckboards that lined the floor were dry. He could see no sign of piping or gas cylinders.

Sergeant Springer gestured to the right. Sam drew his gun, eased off the safety catch and advanced along the trench. He rounded a dogleg corner and found himself face to face with a German soldier.

The German was young, and as startled to see Sam as Sam was to see him. When he caught sight of Sam's pistol, the German threw down his rifle,

raised his hands in the air and exclaimed, '*Kamerad!*
Kamerad! Not shoot, Tommy!'

Sergeant Springer said something in German. The
young soldier nodded vigorously. '*Ja*, Tommy!' he
said. 'Not shoot, Tommy.'

'Why does he keep saying Tommy, Sergeant?' Sam
demanded.

'The Hun call all British troops Tommy, sir,' the
sergeant informed him. 'It's short for Tommy Atkins.'

'Tell him he has to come with us, and tell him
to keep his mouth shut.'

They retraced their steps, walking in single file
with Sam taking the lead and the German soldier
between him and Sergeant Springer. The prisoner
was so anxious to cooperate that he gave Sam a leg-
up when he climbed out of the trench. Sam thanked
him and the German flashed a friendly grin.

Just as they reached the barbed wire, the gunfire
from further down the line ceased.

'Best get a move on, sir,' Sergeant Springer
advised. 'The Hun will be on their way back.'

Sam wriggled through the wire, then the prisoner,
but as Sergeant Springer crawled free, a German flare

went up and the light was like a scream. Sam grabbed the prisoner by the tunic and ran for the wall, with Private Jones and the sergeant bringing up the rear.

German voices called out behind them, followed by rifle shots. Bullets passed above Sam's head, sounding like wet silk being torn. The four men flung themselves behind the cover of the wall. Private Jones began to work the bolt of his rifle.

'Keep your head down, Jones, you bloody fool!' the sergeant barked.

Sam found the whistle that was attached to his belt by a lanyard, placed it between his lips and gave three loud blasts. Hocking and Gray commenced rapid fire, and suddenly bullets were flying everywhere.

'We can't stay here, sir!' shouted Sergeant Springer. 'If they bring up a heavy machine gun, it'll tear the wall apart. We have to run for it.'

'On my count of three then,' said Sam. 'One, two – three!'

They broke cover, running in zigzags as they'd been trained, Sam dragging the stumbling prisoner along with him, bullets smacking into the ground at their feet. When Sam reached the trench, hands reached out to pull him over the sandbags, and as soon as he was on the firing step, he turned to help the German soldier.

Something struck the German, making a noise like an axe striking a log, and he jerked forwards, tumbling onto the floor of the trench. Sam leaped down to examine him. The young soldier's face was as pale as paper and a black stain was spreading rapidly across the breast of his tunic.

'Stretcher-bearers!' Sam roared. 'Stretcher-bearers!'

The German's mouth moved. He took a gargling breath and repeatedly moaned something. Sam bent his head to listen.

'*Mutter,*' said the soldier. '*Mutter. Mutter.*'

Sam glanced up and saw Sergeant Springer. 'What does he want, sergeant?' Sam asked.

'His mother, sir,' said Sergeant Springer. 'He's calling for his mother.'

'Stretcher-bearers!' Sam cried.

'Too late for stretcher-bearers, sir,' the sergeant said gently. 'He's dead. Killed by his own side, poor sod.'

Sam had never seen a corpse before, though he'd heard them described as 'looking peaceful', but the young German didn't look peaceful, only dead. He appeared to have shrunk and something was missing from him, as though he were a Christmas package from which the present had been removed, and at that moment Sam understood death.

Death was the flatness in the German soldier's eyes, the silent stillness of his limbs, the total absence of awareness. The cooling flesh was meat, the body a thing that gave off a sharp stink of emptied bowels and bladder. Death had no honour, no dignity and no purpose.

'Damn this war!' Sam said hoarsely. 'Damn this stupid bloody war!'

Nineteen

On his way back to camp to report to Major Hutchins, Sam suffered a delayed shock reaction and vomited copiously in a communications trench. Houndsome, who was accompanying him, looked away tactfully.

When Sam had finished, he wiped his mouth with the sleeve of his tunic and said, 'Sorry about that, Houndsome.'

'That's all right, sir, you fetch it up. Better out than in,' said Houndsome. 'I reckon as how that meat we had in that stew must have been a bit off.'

'The rum ration, more like,' said Sam. 'That and sheer funk.'

Houndsome hesitated for a moment, then said, 'Sir, that German soldier, the one who got shot. He didn't look much older than what I am, did he?'

'If that.'

'Makes you think, doesn't it, sir?'

'Think what?' said Sam.

Houndsome spoke slowly, struggling to find words for his ideas. 'Well, sir, if young German men and young British men are being killed off in the war, what's going to happen when it's over? Who'll work the land and raise families if all the young men are gone?'

'That's a very good question, Houndsome, but I don't know the answer to it,' said Sam. 'We must pray that it doesn't come to that.'

Camp was crowded with reinforcements for the push. Tents had sprouted like mushrooms everywhere, and supplies were now being stacked in the open and covered with tarpaulins. Major Hutchins' quarters were in a cow shed. One of the stalls had been turned into a makeshift office, with a door supported by wooden trestles acting as a desk. The major was speaking on the telephone, and pointed out a crate for Sam to sit on.

'Yes, sir,' the major said into the receiver. 'Only two casualties so far, a second lieutenant, Erskine, from D company and one private from A company. E and F companies report no gas apparatus present. C company is about to make its report.' He covered the mouthpiece with his hand and said, 'Any gas paraphernalia, Rawnsley?'

Sam shook his head.

The major spoke into the phone again. 'C company found nothing either, sir. I shall – Hello? Hello?' The major rapped the telephone against the table, held it to his ear again, groaned in disgust and placed it in its cradle. 'The blasted wiring's gone again! These things are more trouble than they're worth. What news, Lieutenant, any casualties?'

'We managed to take a prisoner, but he was killed, sir.'

The major shrugged. 'Oh well, it can't be helped. Did you bring his insignia and private effects?'

'Yes, sir,' said Sam. He took a package from his

breast pocket and set it on the desk.

'I'll forward it to intelligence first thing tomorrow,' said the major. He peered closely at Sam. 'You look rather done in, Rawnsley. Was it your first time in action?'

'Yes, sir.'

The major caught something in Sam's tone, leaned back in his chair and said, 'Listen, Rawnsley, I know what you're going through. It's only natural that your first action should leave you feeling shaken up, but it'll pass, believe me. One becomes hardened.'

'Have you ever shot a man, sir?'

The directness of the question took Major Hutchins unawares. 'Good God no! Officers don't shoot the enemy, that's what other ranks are for.'

'I saw a man shot tonight and I don't think that I could do it.'

'Not even for the greater good?'

'I'm no longer convinced that we're fighting for the greater good, sir,' said Sam. 'It seems to me that this war is being fought by the poor to protect the privileges of the rich, and when the fighting's done, nothing will have changed.'

'There you're quite wrong, Lieutenant,' the major said. 'Change is coming. This is an almost inconceivably expensive war. The resources of the Empire are already at full stretch, and there's no sign of an imminent end to the conflict. I believe we're in for the long haul. When the fighting is finally over, the world will be a different place, and Britain's place in it will be different. It will be impossible to return to the old ways.'

'But will it be worth the price, sir?'

'That's not for you or I to know, Rawnsley,' said the major. 'It's our place to do our duty, stick it out and see what happens.'

The night before the attack, Sam didn't find sleep easy to come by. When he eventually managed to doze off, he dreamed about Marion. She was lying in a bed, her hair spread out across the pillow. Her face was as white as aspirin. Next to her bed stood a table. On the table were two bottles of a ruby-coloured liquid and a measuring glass.

Marion smiled and whispered, 'I know you're

there, Sam. I can feel you. Will it be long?'

'No,' Sam told her. 'Not long now.'

On 11th March, dawn broke at six-thirty, bringing with it a flurry of snow that drifted and twirled like ghosts dancing across no man's land. The British trenches were heaving with soldiers, packed together as tightly as rush-hour passengers on an underground train.

At seven-thirty, the four hundred artillery guns of the British barrage opened fire on the enemy line.

Sam had always pictured Hell as being filled with flames, and demons, and the wailing of tormented souls – but Hell was the sound of doors being slammed in the sky, and the ground trembling like jelly, and dark fountains spouting up out of the earth and a sweet-sharp stink of cordite that stung his eyes, nose and throat. Hell relentlessly repeated itself and repeated itself, rupturing time and space, while pale-faced men cowered with their mouths stretched wide to prevent their eardrums from being ruptured by the shock waves from bursting shells.

The bombardment stopped at ten-thirty, and after

the booming came the singing of larks rising into the morning; then voices shouting orders, and the massed clatter of bayonets being fixed.

Captain Charvil smiled at Sam and said, 'Nothing could have lived through that. The artillery chaps have done splendidly, haven't they?'

Sam couldn't think of a polite reply.

Whistles shrilled, and the first line of the attack left the trenches. When they were twenty yards from the German line, the machine guns opened up. Soldiers dropped neatly, one after the other, puppets whose strings had been cut. Some screamed, some twitched, some tried to crawl to safety, but another traverse of machine-gun fire made no man's land quiet and still. A second line went forwards, and a third, and a fourth. The killing wouldn't stop while there were still men to feed to the guns.

Captain Charvil, watching the progress of the battle through binoculars, kept up an excited commentary that made Sam want to throttle him.

'Oh, well done! They've taken the trenches, we've got them on the run.'

'I wouldn't speak too soon, sir,' said Sergeant

Springer. 'The Hun are pulling back to regroup and they're leaving the line clear for their big guns.'

As if to confirm the sergeant's opinion, a shell burst close to the trench, showering down a deluge of small stones and clods of dirt. Sam ducked and kept his head down until the shower had subsided. When he raised his head, he was met by the grinning face of Private Houndsome.

'We were lucky there, sir!' Houndsome said cheerfully. 'If that'd been a few yards closer, we would've—'

DARKNESS.

PART THREE

Twenty

Jill Rawnsley knew the exact moment when Sam died. Just before the pulsing lights of the monitors flattened into straight lines and their blips became monotones, she felt Sam's presence leave, as unmistakeably as if he'd slipped out of the room.

She glanced at Sam, but what was lying in the bed wasn't her son any more, so she turned her eyes to her ex-husband.

His face was expressionless. 'Is that—?' he said. 'Is he—?'

Jill nodded. She was exhausted, relieved – and guilty about feeling relieved. Before long, she knew, there would be nothing but grief, as vast and unyielding as a mountain; but now there was a sense of triumph, as if after a long struggle Sam had completed something and got it right.

She held on to the feeling as she reached for the buzzer above the bed to call a nurse.

Twenty-one

Things seeped into the darkness, marring its perfection; sounds scratched its silence. An awareness grew, sensing first itself, then things beyond – warmth, light, the drone of insects, the rustling of leaves.

Sam opened his eyes. He was on the path by the river, not far from Bankside Cottage. Directly ahead was a wooden stile set into a fence and beyond it stood a small clump of oak trees.

Sam breathed in deeply, savouring the taste of the air. Every cell in his body was alight with life, flowing strong and steady like the current of the river. Marion had kept her promise. His future unfolded, rich in love and closeness, filled with other worlds and other lifetimes.

Something like a blessing descended on him, a feeling of belonging. With his lips stretched into a smile, Sam climbed over the stile and went in search of the toy boat that he knew would be caught in the reeds beside the bank.

Author's Note

There's a very old story, told by the Venerable Bede (AD 673–735) in which an elder compares human life to 'the swift flight of a sparrow through the banqueting hall where you are sitting at dinner on a winter's day . . . Even so, man appears on earth for a little while; but of what went before this life and what follows, we know nothing.' Sam remembers having heard this story, though he thought it was about a swallow, which I think is a better image as a swallow in flight is so beautiful. Also in this country the arrival of swallows marks the beginning of summer, and their departure marks summer's end, and Sam and Marion's story is about beginnings and endings.

Oh, and you really ought to know that Spengler's Syndrome is completely fictional. Thank goodness, there is no such illness in reality.

Andrew Matthews

About the Author

Andrew Matthews read English and Modern History at Reading University before qualifying as a teacher and teaching English for over twenty years. He left teaching in 1994 to concentrate on writing as a full-time career. Married and the owner of several cats, his love of animals has led him to become a member of the UK Wolf Conservation Trust where he has proudly walked with wolves, scratched their stomachs – and been licked by wolves.

When not writing, his other interests include listening to music, astronomy, reading and playing the guitar badly (his own admission!).

His books for the Random House Children's Books lists include *The Breakfast Museum*, *G.S.O.H.* and *From Above with Love*.

Andrew Matthews is extremely pleased to be a part of Children's Literature at this moment in time: 'Children's literature is the most exciting area for a writer,' he says, 'particularly at the moment when there are more gifted writers producing superb work than at any other time. This is the Golden Age of Children's books.'

THE BREAKFAST MUSEUM

Tod stretched out his hands. 'Shall we go and celebrate?'
'Celebrate what?' I asked.
'That we're three unique individuals in a world of clones.'

Andie reckons the Breakfast Museum — a greasy spoon café — is the perfect place to hide out in when her boyfriend dumps her and she spur-of-the-moment bunks off for the day. Only losers and drop-outs go there, don't they?

Wrong! For it's there that Andie meets Tod and Rally and discovers that the Breakfast Museum can provide much more than a plate of egg and chips and something that pretends to be coffee...

A funny, lively tale of heartbreak and hope, roses and romance. You'll wish *you* could find a Breakfast Museum of your own!

'It's really about misfits...and their various problems and preoccupations are explored in a very deftly structured book'
Times Educational Supplement

ISBN 0099 434288